Step
up to the
Plate,
Maria Singh

Step

up to

the

Plate,

Maria Singh

by Uma Krishnaswami

Tu Books

an imprint of Lee & Low Books

New York

TU BOOKS, an imprint of LEE & LOW BOOKS Inc.,
95 Madison Avenue, New York, NY 10016
leeandlow.com

Manufactured in the United States of America
by Worzalla Publishing Company, May 2017

Book design by Sammy Yuen
Book production by The Kids at Our House
The text is set in Minion Pro

10 9 8 7 6 5 4 3 2 1
First Edition

Cataloging-in-Publication Data is on file with the Library of Congress

For Satish

CHAPTER ONE

The Promise of the Morning

"CAN'T, CAN'T, CAN'T," EMILIO TAUNTED.

"Sure I can." Maria gave her little brother a push, but he clung to her like a shadow.

Emilio stuck out his lower lip. He was about to get all pouty and pig-headed, she could tell.

"You're a girl," he said.

"So?" Not for the first time, she wished she did not have a six-year-old hanging on to her like a goatgrass burr.

"Girls can't play ball!"

"Can too. You don't know anything."

Mamá insisted that Emilio was too small to walk to school and back by himself. It was a forty-minute walk if you went fast. In this last month of school, on account of

1

wartime gas rationing, the bus to the farms on the city's outskirts had stopped running.

"I'll tell Papi!" Emilio said. It was always his ultimate weapon.

"You do, and I won't share my tin cans with you."

Emilio glared at Maria, but she knew she'd shut him up, at least for now. Emilio was a pack rat. He collected anything and everything, including cans that could be traded in for ration stamps. He was keen to collect the ration stamps too, except that Mamá took those away from him, needing them to feed the family.

Around them streamed the ragtag morning crowd of Yuba City Public School pupils, chattering and running and bumping into one another. From inside the door, the morning's first bell jangled.

Cut grass and turned dirt scented the air around the school on this warm California morning. Maria wound up her throwing arm the way she'd seen Babe Ruth do in the old newsreel at Smith's Theatre. The one in which the Babe was coaching girls to play ball. The projector got stuck, so the Babe taught the same girl her stance over and over again until even Maria wished he would get on with it and show them how to bat and Papi was about ready to burst from exasperation. Maria could remember every word Babe Ruth said.

Wind up. Wind up. Follow your arm right through. An easy play is hard to make.

She gripped her imaginary ball with both hands. She pulled back and let it fly.

"Maria!" It was Connie. Consuelo Khan, biggest and bossiest of the seven-count-'em-seven Khan kids. Connie to everyone.

Maria and Connie were friends forever. They'd thrown balls at each other and swung at them with dime-store bats since they were six years old. Both of them came from half-and-half families here in Yuba City, with mothers from Mexico and fathers from faraway India.

People called the families Mexican Hindus even though the fathers were mostly either Sikh or Muslim in the God department. The families joked that they were adha-adha, which meant "half and half." The fathers had come from India during famine or war and then found themselves in these strange United States, forbidden to marry outside their race, unable to go back. This was the history, and everyone knew it.

"You going to stay to sign up, right?" Connie said.

"Oh yes." Maria pushed all the objections out of her mind. Pushed her entire family away, Papi and Mamá and Emilio parroting Papi.

"Good," Connie said. "Go on, chica, don't dawdle." She shoved the littlest of the Khan kids through the door.

"Papi's never letting you." Emilio had found his gumption again. He hopped and skipped ahead of Maria, singing, "Never, never, never! He'll never let you play!"

"Quit it, Emilio!" Yet secretly, Maria's heart turned over.

Papi's never gonna let you. It was true, wasn't it? Even after all his years in America, even with a wife from Mexico, Maria's papi carried too much of his native India within him. She knew only too well that in his old-fashioned view, girls did not wear shorts and run around on ball fields.

Connie shot her a sympathetic glance, shrugged, and vanished through the school door behind her brothers and sisters.

Maria appealed to Emilio. "I gotta stay behind after school. Don't tell Papi and Mamá. Just stay and wait for me, okay?"

"What about Tía Manuela?"

"You can't tell her either."

"I mean," he insisted, "she's coming today. Tía is."

Maria's heart gave a little guilty lurch. How could she have forgotten? Their sweet auntie, Mamá's baby sister. Softball signup had pushed Tía Manuela clean out of Maria's mind. She pulled herself together. "We'll be home before then. She never comes till late anyway."

He scrunched his nose up at her.

"Don't tell, okay?" She tried not to sound desperate.

He gave her a sly look. "Will you give me half of your tin cans?" Behind the bathhouse at home was a pile of cans waiting to be salvaged. Papi said tin cans were going to war to help America, although Maria was not sure how that worked exactly. You could turn them in for ration stamps. That much she knew. It was as good as getting cash for your trash.

Emilio loved holding the ration stamps in his hands and poring over the designs on each one. He was mad about those stamps even though he had to give up every last one when he got home. Mamá and Papi counted them diligently and traded them in for sugar and butter and gasoline. "Half your tin cans, huh, Maria?" Emilio prompted.

She considered. "And if I don't?"

He stuck his tongue out at her. Maria made a grab for him, but he scooted inside, ducking past the teacher stationed in the hallway, waiting, ruler in hand, to swipe at the legs of children who dared to run.

CHAPTER TWO

US

SOMEHOW MARIA MADE IT THROUGH THE SCHOOL day, through multiplication tables and spelling, managing to find her place in the latest copy of *My Weekly Reader*. Someone had drawn a baseball bat and ball in the margin. It was surely a sign.

"Maria," cautioned Miss Newman, looking over her shoulder. "That is class property."

"Miss Newman, I never—" Maria protested. "It was there already."

"Please erase it," said Miss Newman mildly. Before Maria could say another word in her defense—she hadn't, she wouldn't, truly, she never—Miss Newman said, "Read the first story, Maria."

Maria swallowed her indignation and read. "'A few

weeks ago, a soldier in Africa was given a medal for bravery. This soldier was a woman. She is one of the WACs who have gone to Africa.'"

A woman? Injustice receded, and wounded pride as well. Women could be soldiers? They could? No kidding! According to My Weekly Reader, General Eisenhower said women were among his best soldiers.

Then Maria came to a line that stopped her short. *They do not fight, of course.*

"Go on," Miss Newman said.

"'They do not fight, of course.'" Maria picked the reading up again, but then she had to blurt out, "So how are they soldiers, then?" The weight of the puzzling world came down on her as it did sometimes when she wasn't expecting it.

Miss Newman paused to consider. "That is an interesting question," she said at last. "It is a fact, I believe. They don't fight. Should they, or shouldn't they?" Other teachers asked questions to get the right answers out of their pupils. Miss Newman loved to ask questions for which there were either no answers or far too many answers. "What do you think?" she asked them.

A hubbub broke out, with the girls divided: "Why not?" "Never!" "Would you want to?"

The boys wasted no time on words. They shifted into the Movietone News soundtrack, whining high and long like shells landing, imitating the ack-ack-ack of machine gun fire just the way you might hear it at the cinema.

Miss Newman had to thump the ink blotter on her desk to restore order, but it made her smile, where other teachers scolded and threatened and did not care to invite students' opinions in the first place. "Maria, will you read on, please," said Miss Newman.

The noise quieted. *Would I want to fight, myself?* Maria thought, trying to imagine such a scenario and failing. Why would anyone want to fight in a war? It felt unreal, something from the movies that should not be happening in real life. She read along, her mind in a whirl.

The WACs in England, she read, had to go to language school to learn English telephone ways. They learned that when they heard "You are through" it didn't mean they needed to stop talking and hang up. It meant they could start talking.

That is strange, for sure, Maria thought. Are they

not supposed to speak English the same as in America? Not like Mamá from Mexico and Papi from India who might be excused for having grown up with completely different languages.

Somehow she made it to the end of the page. "'Strain all waste fats—'"

Everyone laughed.

Wait. That wasn't part of the article; it was just a message at the end telling people to save all their waste kitchen fat so the government could use it for the war effort.

This was a good war, wasn't it? Everyone said it was necessary. Hitler made it so.

"Thank you," said Miss Newman. "Boys and girls, do you know that next week, in San Francisco, delegates from forty-six countries are meeting in a conference? It is the United Nations Conference on International Organization. Their goal is to fashion a way that we can end wars and promote peace." Miss Newman thought that children should know what was going on in the world around them. She was always throwing news like this at her class, whether any of it stuck or not.

"Did we defeat the Jerries already?" Tim Singh called out. He'd been asking every day for the last six months.

"Don't forget the Japs," Elizabeth Becker said, two rows behind Maria. "They're attacking us in Asia."

Maria winced. Elizabeth's stuck-up voice always had that effect on her. Her daddy owned the land that Papi farmed, and both girls knew it.

"We will say 'Japanese' in this classroom, please," Miss Newman said. "And 'Germans' too."

Elizabeth's head jerked up. She looked as if she wanted to say something but then changed her mind. *Why*, Maria wondered, *does all this matter so much to Elizabeth?* What did it matter what you called the enemy?

"No, the war is not yet over," Miss Newman said, "but President Truman has said he will carry on as he believes President Roosevelt would have done." Most adults raised their voices when they meant for you to listen. Miss Newman lowered hers, yet every word carried as she walked up and down the aisles between the desks. "Do we all know what President Roosevelt believed about ending this war?"

Silence.

"Our late president believed it possible for nations to stop fearing one another and live in peace. Do you not remember my telling you this last week?"

"Yes, Miss Newman," the class chorused. It was best to agree with her when she strode like that between the desks.

Not everyone joined in the chorus. Next to Maria, Janie Gill clamped her mouth shut and said nothing. Her daddy was at war somewhere in France. They hadn't heard from him in months, which may have accounted for Janie not believing that things like peace were possible.

From behind Maria, Elizabeth muttered, "Who cares?" prompting Miss Newman to declare that was quite enough, thank you very much.

Maria sighed. In less than a week, so much had happened. Roosevelt had died. The presidency had changed hands. And when would it end, this faraway war that had begun when Maria was only four? It threatened to go on forever.

Sometimes, when she stopped to think about it, it seemed to Maria that Hitler was reason enough to be fighting this war, because you wouldn't want a bad man like that to win, would you? If Hitler won, he'd be in charge here in America and that would not be good. Everyone said he was a madman. Still, mostly Hitler was as thin and invisible as Papi's India or Mamá's native Mexico.

And now it seemed in the middle of this war there were

also women. Women in the WACs in Africa and women on the home front. Hadn't Maria's own Tía Manuela left Yuba City and gone away to Los Angeles, where she worked for the Lockheed plant that made planes? Making planes—what a big, strange idea. Maria had never been in a plane, nor had anyone she knew. She thought of Tía Manuela working in that factory, turning rivets and fastening bolts. It made her feel as if life itself was turning into a Movietone newsreel.

So girls on the ball field was not such a crazy idea. Was it?

CHAPTER THREE

Playing Ball

ON THE LAST CLANG OF THE DAY'S LAST BELL, MARIA tore out the door and around the building to the dirt field in back of the school. It was not much of a ball field. The sun blazed down on it. The wind whipped the dust up. Rocks tripped you up if you weren't careful. Weeds choked out the thin grass. It was the only field there was. The way girls were streaming over that grass today, you'd think it was ladies' day at some major-league stadium.

But where was Connie? She was nowhere in sight. Finally, Maria spotted her running around the corner and across the field, her feet kicking up dust.

"Where were you?" Maria cried. "What took you so long?"

"Stopped to change," Connie explained. She wore a pair

of cream-colored shorts. "Mamá made them for me. What do you think?"

The truth was that Maria wished she had a pair. She swallowed that thought. Instead she said, "They're nice." Connie grinned at her, and Maria had to smile back.

"You think there's enough of us?" said Janie Gill, tugging a thread from the frayed edge of her sleeve. Could her mamá not fix that shirt?

"Do we need ten players, or nine, or what?" Milly Anderson asked. She'd come with her cousins Sal and Joyce.

Alternates as well, right? What if someone got hurt? No one knew for sure. Miss Newman's words had drawn them all here. *In Yuba City Union High they are putting girls' teams together, but there is nothing for younger ones. It's my dream that here in Sutter County our young girls can play ball.*

It wasn't official even. Not like a league or anything. Nothing like that. Miss Newman was just doing this because she wanted to.

The girls showed up anyway, because they wanted to play. Look at them all! Lucy and Dot Garcia, Milly and Sal and Joyce. And look who else! Elizabeth Becker.

Oh. Elizabeth. A small cold knot settled into Maria's

heart at the sight. Did Elizabeth want to play? She'd never seemed interested whenever they'd played catch before. Elizabeth wore a smart blue gym suit. It had a sailor collar bordered in white, with navy seed stitches around the edge, and oh! Those ankles! Elizabeth had on bobby socks to match her perfect clothes. In a hundred years, Mamá would never let Maria get a pair, for fear they would turn her into a mad teenager before her time.

Maria's old yellow dress suddenly chafed at the collar. Its twice-lengthened hem drooped on her. Its cloth had worn thin from repeated washing. No gym suit for her. No. Papi believed girls should be ladylike and wear dresses— good long ones, moreover, that covered up most of their legs. And when Papi got stubborn like that, nothing could shake him.

Elizabeth was laughing and joking with the Anderson girls as if Maria was not worth her notice. Milly smiled and tried to make room for Connie and Maria. She was friendly with everyone even though she came from an old Sutter County family and could have put on airs.

Elizabeth glanced at Connie. "New shorts," she said. "Did you make them yourself?"

"No. My mom did."

Elizabeth turned to Milly. She whispered, "From a pillowcase, I'll bet."

Milly said nothing. Connie looked crushed.

"Come on, Connie." Maria grabbed her friend's hand. "Miss Newman's ready for us."

The girls clustered around Miss Newman and her clipboard. Janie's cousins Suze and Didi arrived to join them. "Six, seven, eight . . ." Miss Newman said. "Do we have nine? Wait." She turned to a couple of newcomers in exasperation. "Did I not tell you this was for girls? Are you girls?"

Four boys had shown up. Tim Singh, Charley and Joey Hamilton, and Connie's cousin, Mondo Khan. The ruffians shook their heads, but they stayed to watch regardless.

"We have eleven," said Miss Newman, turning her back upon the boys. "If you are serious, the eleven of you could form a team—ten, plus one alternate. There will be other girls' teams in the county. We could play teams from Marysville, from Stockton even. Imagine that."

Imagine. It was a dream, all right.

The watching boys jostled each other for room and bragged in loud, proud voices. "We can pound you girls into the dust, see if we can't."

"Oh, take a powder!" yelled Connie, who had recovered from Elizabeth's jibe.

Snooty Elizabeth didn't hoot at the boys. *Not because she's on our side*, Maria thought. *Elizabeth despises most of us. She thinks she is too good for us.*

Miss Newman shuffled them into two lines to practice throwing. "Just to warm you up," she said. She handed out softballs from a leather satchel. "Got a few gloves in here as well, and a catcher's mitt." She had drawn a diamond with chalk lines in the dirt. The lines had a few wobbles in them, but there they were.

"Home plate." Miss Newman pointed to the battered tin plate she'd hammered into the ground at one end. There were snickers all around. "I know, I know," Miss Newman said. "We'll have to make do."

"Who we going to play, Miss Newman?"

"What are we going to call ourselves?"

"Whoa, whoa, whoa!" said Miss Newman. "First things first. "We'll set up our bases later, but for now, show me how you throw a ball."

They showed her. Hands spun. Feet flew in all directions. The balls thudded in front of the line of girls. Not a one went far enough to hit home plate. A couple of them made it more than a few feet. Miss Newman laughed. "I see," she said. "We have work to do. Come on now, let's see some proper stances."

She showed them how to throw a ball as she talked to them about the All-American Girls Softball League. "They used to be a softball league," she said, "but now they are going to change their name. And their game as well. But you . . ." She took one step back, then swung her arm back and then forward in an arc, holding the ball so everyone could see. "You will pitch underhand. See? Step. Step out with the foot that's opposite your throwing arm. Then swing that arm back. Then forward. Like a pendulum. And . . . let the ball go." The ball landed way past home base. Lucy ran to retrieve it.

"Not like this?" Maria swung into the routine she'd memorized courtesy of Movietone.

"That is baseball," Miss Newman said. "We will play softball. Here. Try." She held the ball out to Maria.

Maria tried it. She stepped out with her opposite foot. Then let her arm swing like a pendulum, backward and forward, letting the ball release. Something lit up inside her.

"Well done," said Miss Newman. She handed out

gloves. They would have to share, and there was none for Connie, who was left-handed.

Miss Newman asked the girls to help her set out the bases. Then she had them line up and walk across the field from third base to first, picking up as many rocks as they could and heaping them up by the fence. All the time, she talked to them. Maria was swept into the game by Miss Newman's words—"fair ground and foul" and "the distance from the pitcher's plate to home plate" and more, so much more. Out in the world, grown-up women were playing baseball. Here in Maria's own world, the ball could spin, electric, from her fingertips.

Miss Newman was a whirlwind, checking everyone's feet as she taught them how to pitch. "Head over shoulders, nice solid position. Too far apart, Janie, you won't get any speed on the ball that way . . . too close together, Connie, Didi. There is a time to be a lady, but I am telling you this is not it." She showed them how to follow through with hands and wrists, how to release that ball, what to do with their elbows and knees. "The arm stays nice and tight as you throw. That's it, that's it!"

They took turns in pairs. The balls flew wide and far. As the players scrambled to catch them, they mussed up Miss Newman's chalk lines.

"With any luck," said Miss Newman, "in the next couple of years, this town will have a real ball field for us all."

A real ball field? It seemed the city was considering using a piece of land for exactly that. For young ball players. *That would be us*, thought Maria. It was purely dizzying.

"Step out, step out," Miss Newman called. "Out, all the way—wide and easy. That's right. Watch," said Miss Newman. All the girls paused in their own throwing as Miss Newman pointed at Maria. "Try a rise ball now, let it peel out nice and easy. Look at my hand. Like turning a doorknob. Ready, Maria? Go ahead!"

Maria's ball flew out. She could feel the difference. She could feel the ball leaving her fingers. One more time and once again. It wasn't perfect, but she could control it. Every little turn of her wrist made a difference. With every pitch, something hummed inside Maria.

After pitching for a while, they practiced passing the ball to each other. Maria was caught up in the rhythm of it. Only once, when her hand brushed her skirt, was she reminded of her dress. She could almost fool herself into believing it didn't matter so much.

"Good work," Miss Newman said. "Now let's see how well you can field. I'm going to hit some grounders and you can take turns fielding them. Let's go!" The girls lined up farther out, past the marks for bases, and Miss Newman stood at the place they'd designated home base. She pointed to her left—the girls' right—and said, "Watch me now. There's left field." Pointed to the center. "That's center field. To my right is . . ."

"Right field," they chorused.

"You got it. It's all based on what's left and right from this direction. That does not change, no matter where you are." She took out a bat from the pile of equipment she'd hauled along. She made the girls toss their balls to *her*. *Smack! Smack!* Her bat connected sharply with each one.

The lumpy old leather gloves passed between the girls. First Janie, then Maria, Connie, Lucy, Elizabeth, Dot, Sal, Milly, Didi, Joyce, Suze. Lucy was their surprise fielder. Shy and quiet in long blue pants, with a white shirt tucked firmly into the waistband, she had an eagle eye, and she was fierce. There wasn't a ball that was going to get past her.

Since Connie didn't have a glove that fit, she just wore

the right-handers' glove. She tossed and caught, both with her left hand, pulling the glove off in between. Miss Newman sighed and shook her head, but Connie's antics made everyone smile.

Some of the girls were better than the rest. Didi had never played before, but she was so good-humored and happy to be there that no one held it against her.

"Your turn, Maria," Miss Newman said.

Maria got into ready position, crouching, her left hand in the old glove with its worn leather wristband. The ball whizzed out and she ran, low to the ground.

"Square to the ball," Miss Newman said. "Keep your eye on it. Use both hands."

Maria kept her eye on the ball. She kept her hand low, low, low, and there . . . it . . . came.

And then—whoops! The twice-lengthened hem of Maria's skirt got between her legs. She tugged at it, tried to pull her dress straight and reach for the ball at the same time. She fumbled and missed. Somewhere in the dust behind her, the ball rolled to a stop. Somewhere on the edge of the dirt field, the boys' laughter rang out. It sounded like jeers.

And just like that, the dizzy joy of this day evaporated

into disgrace and humiliation. Maria hardly knew how she endured the rest of practice, but finally the hour and a half was past. "You're doing fine, my dear," said Miss Newman when they were through, "but you must speak with your parents about getting more suitable clothes. Shorts, I think, are best for practice."

Before Maria could make herself scarce, Connie caught up with her. "Hi, Maria."

"Hi," Maria said. She cast a sideways look at Connie in her pillowcase shorts. Maria asked, "Your daddy said okay to you wearing shorts?"

Connie waved her hands in a *yes and no* kind of way. "He didn't like it," she said, "but Mamá talked him into it."

Oh. So why couldn't Maria's Mamá do that? Not for the first time in her life, Maria wished her parents didn't always agree with one another about everything. It's all or nothing with them, she thought gloomily. You could never get just one of them on your side; if you wanted an ally, you had to talk them both into it.

"You want a pair?" said loyal Connie. "I got an extra."

Maria considered. Did she want Connie's shorts? It was a generous offer. But if she said yes, she'd have to hide those shorts from Papi and Mamá.

It was the length of the shorts Papi objected to—showing so much leg. A kacha would be all right, he said. That was the underwear—like long shorts—that people of Papi's Sikh religion were supposed to wear. Maria and Emilio each had a pair, and wore them whenever they went to the Sikh temple. Papi would want to know why she couldn't just wear her kacha to play ball. Better yet, with her skirt over it? Why would that be embarrassing? He didn't understand. It was all very complicated, and the more Maria thought about it the more impossible it all became.

"So?" asked Connie. "Want 'em?"

From somewhere inside Maria a small lie raised its head. It made her feel better, so she spoke it out loud. "Nah," she said. "It's all right. I'll ask Mamá. She'll sew me a pair." And she added the thing that she wasn't being, just then. "Honest."

CHAPTER FOUR

Honest

THE LIE THAT HAD SLIPPED SO LIGHTLY FROM Maria's lips now buzzed in her mind like a cloud of mosquitoes. She couldn't just ask Mamá to sew her a pair of shorts! Mamá would immediately tell Papi and Papi would say a big fat No. No shorts and therefore no playing ball, because you had to have shorts to play. He'd said no once and he'd say it again, which was why she'd tried to play in her dress, and look how that turned out! Asking Mamá was not going to be so easy, was it? How Maria wished that just saying a thing out loud could make it true.

But she didn't have too much time to think about all this because she just that moment remembered something she was supposed to have remembered all along. Emilio. Where was he? She looked around for him, but he wasn't waiting for her like she'd told him to. "Did you see Emilio?" she asked Connie.

"He went home," Connie said. "He went with the rest of the kids. I saw him."

Oh no! Emilio was supposed to wait for her. Now he'd get home by himself and Mamá would want to know why.

Connie was chattering away. Wasn't it exciting, the promise of the new ball field? "The land's been deeded already," Connie said.

Maria tried to quiet her buzzing mind as they walked toward the Feather River Bridge. "What does that mean, deeded?" she asked.

Connie explained that the land had been given to the county. "It means they have to use it for public works."

Public works. That sounded important. Did a ball field count? Was it public works? But they couldn't talk anymore because there was Elizabeth, standing on the thin grass by the roadside beyond the schoolyard.

"Aren't you going home?" asked Connie.

"My dad's coming to get me," Elizabeth said.

At least they wouldn't have to walk home with her.

"He's just gone into town to pick up his new car," said Elizabeth.

"You'll need extra gasoline coupons, huh?" Maria tried to keep her words nice and polite. Mamá and Papi were always complaining that between the John Deere tractor and the truck there were never enough gas coupons to get by. But then, Mamá and Papi had to hand over half of what they made each harvest to Mr. Becker for the lease of their farmland.

Elizabeth shrugged. She tossed her chestnut curls. She said, "Makes no difference. You can always get gas if you're willing to pay for it."

"That's black market!" Connie shot Maria a look. Their fathers both had very definite opinions about black marketeers who sold meat, sugar, and gasoline on the sly. Those were things you were supposed to use less of so they could be sent to soldiers on the war front. Selling them to make a profit was more than illegal. It was downright wicked.

Elizabeth laughed. "Black, white, khaki—who cares?"

Maria was dumbfounded. Did that mean Elizabeth's daddy bought gas on the black market? Papi said people like that should go to jail.

"Daddy says he can't wait for the war to be over," Elizabeth said, "so we can start making cars again in

America. He had to buy a 1941 model, would you believe?"

"Um—no," said Maria, who had not in her entire life given the buying of cars a single thought.

A truck came chugging along the road.

"All the car companies are making military vehicles," Elizabeth said. "There's not a new car on the market, Daddy says . . ." Her words were drowned out by the approaching engine.

It was a large Chevy truck, slowing down to pass them. The words United States Army Air Force were stenciled along the side.

"Germans," Connie said. "From Camp Beale!"

There were men sitting on benches in the truck bed. Maria could see them peering between the canvas flaps. She could see their eyes, could feel them upon her. She looked away hastily. Trucks like this one hauled German prisoners of war around each morning to work on orchards and farms for a low wage. In the afternoon, back they would go to the camp.

Elizabeth's face had turned chalky white.

"It's okay, really," Maria said. "Nothing to worry about."

"They have guards and everything," Connie added.

The truck disappeared in a flurry of dust.

"I hate it." Elizabeth's voice trembled. "I hate it all."

"The war, you mean?" Connie said.

"Nobody likes it," said Maria.

"Maybe the Germans like it," Connie said. "But we don't."

"Stop!" said Elizabeth. "Just stop it."

Connie gave Maria another look as if to *say, Quit trying to figure this one out*. "I gotta go home," Connie said.

Maria nodded. Enough was enough.

They said hurried good-byes and left Elizabeth waiting for her father to pick her up in his fancy car.

Connie muttered, "That Elizabeth!"

"She's jumpy today," Maria said. "I can't imagine why."

"I'd be jumpy too with a daddy like that," Connie said.

That was true. Arnold Becker wore a constant scowl. Out of Mamá and Papi's hearing, Maria and Emilio called him "oso" because he looked like a big, scary bear.

They had arrived at the bus stop. Ahead of them, roads peeled away to the farmlands on both sides of the river. People converged on the intersection, some walking across the bridge, others coming from town. Lots of people walked or rode bikes these days because of gas rationing.

"Gotta go." Connie waved and ran down the weedy

slope behind the bus stop, onto the dirt road before the bridge. To the west lay the Khan place. Maria's family lived on the east side, across the river.

Gravel crunched beneath Maria's feet as she walked across the bridge. The river reminded her of Tía Manuela. Tía had told her it once had a Spanish name, Rio de las Plumas, because some old-time explorer had fancied he saw feathers floating on the water.

"Fancied? Did he see 'em or didn't he?" Maria had asked.

"Doesn't matter," Tía Manuela had said. "What matters is the name." Rio de las Plumas. So sweet, like a song. The English name, Feather River, made it sound like an old pillow.

Today the water in the river was sluggish and churning with brown mud brought down from faraway mountains. Maria hurried across the bridge. Tía was probably already at home. Everyone would wonder where Maria was.

Only wait! Who was that hurrying toward her? She knew that voice, crying "Hola, Maria!" She'd recognize that stride anywhere.

Maria shrieked with delight. "Tía Manuela!"

It was, it was. Maria's auntie herself, suitcase in hand, dressed up to visit in a smart two-tone dress with shutter pleats and a button front.

"I been calling you ever since I spotted you, niñita! Thought you'd never hear me!" She set the suitcase down and opened both arms wide.

Maria ran gratefully into her hug. "Tía!"

Mamá's baby sister, Maria's favorite aunt, was all comfort and laughter and the clean smell of Lux soap. "I'm off to catch my bus," she said. "Just came from visiting your mommy, so where have you been, my darling?"

Maria gaped. "You're going back to work already?" What a short visit! Oh, Mamá would be real mad now.

Tía Manuela nodded. "Come on. Want to walk back to the bus stop with me?"

"Okay."

Tía explained her rush. "Couldn't get an overnight pass, so it's a flying visit. I sent you a postcard."

"It hasn't come yet."

"I know, chica, Hortensia said so. You watch for it in a day or two, okay?"

"How's the airplane factory?" Maria asked.

"Let me tell you, that's some work we're doing these days." Tía Manuela had to make sure that every nut was tightened, every bolt fastened, nothing was overlooked, nothing was where it shouldn't be.

"If it wasn't for you," Maria said, "those planes could fall apart when they fly."

Tía Manuela laughed. "Yes, m'ijita, there's lots of us working the assembly lines." She held her hand out. "See these calluses?" Her palm was ridged and tough. "From the bucking bar. The riveter shoots the rivet in, and I get to smooth it out on the other side. Feel that muscle?"

Maria prodded her arm. Solid, like the steel of a plane. "You got that from bucking too?"

Tía Manuela nodded. "Don't get me wrong. I'm not saying war's a good thing, but you know what? This war's been the best thing that could happen to many women. Come on. Walk me to the bus station."

Maria carried her purse for her while Tía Manuela hefted the suitcase easily. The bus was pulling in.

"How is the war a good thing?" Maria asked. "For anyone?"

Tía Manuela said, "Well, think about me. I put on my pants every day and I take my lunch pail to work. I do a man's job."

Maria stopped in her tracks. "Pants?" she said. "You wear pants to work?"

Her aunt laughed. "I couldn't do what I do in this dress,

now, could I? Hortensia told me about your little problem with your Papi," she said. "Don't let it stop you, honey. Don't you let nothing stop you. Promise me."

"I promise." Maria's heart grew wings.

One last hug, and her aunt joined the line of people waiting for the bus. The conductor began taking tickets, and boarding commenced. That bus would go down to Marysville, then turn away to the southwest. It would drive through farmlands and wasteland and into the darkness and all the way to Los Angeles, where Tía Manuela fixed rivets in place with a bucking bar and had become a new woman.

She waved at Maria, blew kisses from the bus window. Maria turned away to go home, wishing Mamá's sister didn't have to be so far away.

Walking home in the light of the April evening, Maria held Tía Manuela's last hug close in her mind, and with it the spring-fresh confidence of Lux soap.

CHAPTER FIVE

Chasing Trouble

WHEN MARIA GOT HOME, EMILIO WAS CHASING THE chickens in the yard, his hair sticking up in the back of his head the way it always did when Mamá had just recently cut it. "You're in trouble," he sang to Maria. "Mamá's gonna get you!" He stomped his feet at the rooster, sending him flapping.

"You didn't wait for me!" Maria scolded.

He blinked at her. "Oh. I forgot."

"Never mind. You didn't tell, did you?"

"No! Didn't I promise you? Mamá asked where you were and I said you were with Connie and them, that's all. Will you gimme your cans?"

"Shh." They were on the steps of the house now and she didn't want Mamá to know about the deal with the cans. If

Mamá knew, it would all come out and that would be the end of playing ball. "Quiet!"

He stood his ground. *Gimme your cans,* he mouthed back.

"Oh, just take 'em," she hissed at him. "Only half, okay?"

He whooped in delight and ran down the steps and around the house, toward the shed that housed the outhouse and the bathhouse. Behind that shed was the precious pile of cans.

"You're late," Mamá called from the kitchen, just as soon as Maria got her body through the front door. "Manuela came and went already."

Maria tried to take it on the chin. "I know," she said, putting her book bag on the steps and breathing deeply before she entered the kitchen. "I'm sorry."

Mamá pounced at once. "How do you know?"

"I met her on the road, Mamá."

"You did?"

"Yes. I helped her with her bags."

"Not all evening you didn't," Mamá grumbled, but already she was calming down. "Did she catch the bus?"

Maria nodded. "I waited till it left."

"And before that?"

Oh no. What did that mean? "Huh?" If she could only still her guilty heart.

"You know perfectly well," Mamá said. "How come Emilio walked back by himself?"

Maria's heart gave a pounding leap. "Sorry, Mamá." She hesitated. "I was playing." Well, that part was true. Literally true. Just not the whole truth.

"Playing?" Mamá said. "With who?"

"Connie." That was true too. Wasn't it?

Mamá sighed. She looked up at the ceiling as if she was asking God and the archangels for guidance. But all she said was, "When he's older, he can come home on his own. It's only a few weeks left for the end of school now, Maria. You hear me?"

"Sí, Mamá."

"I'm getting dinner ready," Mamá said. "Help me." She plunked vegetables down on the old chopping block. "Take the little knife."

As Maria opened the drawer that held knives and kitchen utensils, she avoided catching the eye of the plaster statue on the shelf above. The shelf served as a kitchen altar. On it, for all of Maria's life, had stood the Lady of Guadalupe, blessed Mother of Jesus, two and a half feet tall with her pleated robes and sweet face. Like a conscience dressed in blue, because wasn't she, Maria, named for this very saint?

At the feet of the statue was a book—Papi's prayer book with yellowing pages that he turned once a week, reading under his breath, making the kitchen hum with the strange yet familiar tones of his Punjabi language. Next to the book was a wooden carving of the holy man who had founded Papi's Sikh religion hundreds of years ago (although not as many hundreds as Jesus and Mary and Joseph). A rounded symbol was worked into the wood like a winged letter. Papi said it was called Ikonkar, which meant "There is one God."

Oh, the altar was a reminder of Maria's lies, deceit, and trickery.

"Don't waste the cilantro," Mamá said. "Throw the stems in as well. It all tastes good."

"Sí, Mamá." Maria chopped cilantro and peeled onions for Mamá's tamales. Mamá gave her a suspicious look or two, but held her peace.

Maria's eyes watered. Maybe it was onions and maybe it was conscience. She wondered how it was that Mamá could not hear her heart beating, as loud as it thudded in her own two ears.

•••

School began the next day with a bribe, plain and simple. "I'll give you a penny if you wait for me. Wait until I'm done with ball practice, okay?"

"And if I don't?"

She made a scary face at him. "Okay, okay," Emilio said. "I'll wait for you."

Rumors flew that day. Connie lobbed the first one. "That truck!" she whispered over the squeak of their folding seats. "Did you hear?"

"No, what?"

"Three men. Three. Can you believe?" Connie waggled three fingers under their connected desks so only Maria could see. "Escaped. From Camp Beale."

"You're kidding me." Maria shuddered. She could almost feel those eyes peering at her through the wooden slats of the truck. Escaped prisoners were dangerous, weren't they? Maybe even armed. Roaming the countryside. But somewhere mixed in with the terror of it there was also a thrill. Escaped prisoners were the stuff of news, spilling into the kitchen over the crackling and screeching of the old RCA radio. Who ever thought such people could leap right out of the news and into real life?

Connie was not kidding. "Maybe we saw them,"

she said. "Maybe they were in that same truck."

"No more chatter, girls," said Miss Newman, turning to the green chalkboard, chalk in hand. The morning's arithmetic problem scratched itself onto the board and Maria groaned her way into it. A beekeeper has sixty-eight hives and checks each one five times a year . . .

Why sixty-eight? she wondered, annoyed. She dug her pencil into the paper, wishing she could just let the bees out, let them sting that man and put an end to her torture. She forced herself to address the multiplication sum.

Math hour went by. So did history and geography and English and all the other tedious hours that made up the day.

At recess, Connie wanted to know, "Did you get shorts yet?"

Maria had to admit, no, she hadn't. She half hoped that Connie would offer her a pair again, but Connie just said, "Ask your Papi for long pants. Maybe he'll let you play in long pants."

"Yeah," Maria said. "Maybe." She tucked the idea away for later. Oh, how stubborn they were, these fathers from Punjab. Did girls in India not play any sports, and if they did, what on earth did they wear?

At the end of that day—oh joy!—came the bell that

Maria had longed for. And in no time at all, there she was, running, running to the field in the back where the girls gathered. She looked around to make sure Emilio was still there. He was chasing crickets in the tangled shade of an old pear tree. She waved at him and then proceeded to forget about him, because there was Connie, yelling, "Come here, Maria! Look what I found!"

A glove. Connie had found a glove that fit. It was a bit ratty but still, an honest-to-goodness ball-player's glove for a lefty, with webbing and a button-down strap across the back of the hand. Its red-brown leather smelled of sawdust.

Today it was drill, drill, drill, and nobody wasted time. Not even Elizabeth dared to dawdle.

"For now," said Miss Newman, "we'll work on technique." For now, too, Miss Newman gave Maria's dress a sideways look but said nothing about it.

Somebody asked about the new ball field.

"There may not be one," said Miss Newman, "if we can't show them that we have enough teams able to make good use of it. Now let's throw some balls." She had them work in pairs again, pitching and catching.

Then she had them pitch to her, one by one, while she herself batted.

Maria held the ball—three fingers and a thumb—and when she released it, it sang out fast and free. Whack! Miss Newman smacked it clear into left field.

"Gotcha," said Miss Newman. "Throw five days a week and you'll learn when to release the ball." She showed the girls how to take a stance, face the batter, count one thousand and one, and throw, throw, throw. "Figure out your batter," she said. "Give her what she doesn't expect."

All afternoon the girls took turns pitching and fielding and catching the ball in the outfield while Miss Newman swung the bat. Then she pitched and they lined up to bat. "Feel that bat. Heft that bat," Miss Newman called. "Move your hands up. Choke up on the bat. Feel what's right for you. Aaaaand—let's go, go, go!"

The balls flew fast and hard. Maria clutched the bat. Whoosh! She swung. "Do not hit from the hip pocket!" cried Miss Newman. "Or that ball will be in the catcher's mitt before you can even bring your bat into position. Look. Let me show you how."

She made Maria pitch to her. "Watch me," she said. She pulled the bat back no farther than her ear. "Elbows out. Flexed wrists, loosen up those muscles."

Slowly, slowly, the ball began to feel like part of Maria's body. When she released it, she could feel it flying off her fingertips. Her body and the ball were one.

Miss Newman made Janie pitch to Maria. She corrected them as she went. She showed them different ways a player can change up her pitch so the batter doesn't know what's coming. It was hard work and it did not all come easy. But was it good? Oh, it was magical.

They ended with what Miss Newman called a round drill: One player on each base, the rest lined up at short-stop. Miss Newman hit a grounder to Janie, who was up first at shortstop. Janie threw it to Maria at first base, then followed her throw by running to first. Maria caught the ball, threw it to Dot at second base and ran to second. Dot caught, threw to third, and so on.

Everyone was fielding, throwing, and running, all in one drill, and everyone, everyone was moving all the time.

The next ball came, and the next. *It's like a dance*, Maria thought in a daze. *It is a thing of beauty*. But her attention had wavered. She fumbled the ball. She tried to recover, but it had already touched the ground.

"Easy now," said Miss Newman. "Secure the ball before you try to throw. Pay attention, Maria."

In a blink, the beauty of the day crumbled to dust.

For the rest of practice, Maria ran the whole thing through her mind. She played it just the way the announcer ran his commentary out into the air on that old Babe Ruth movie she'd seen at Smith's Theatre. In this version, it did not go so well. *And Maria Singh's at third base and oh, she takes her eye off the ball. It glances off her glove. It bounces. She manages to snatch it up but that was a bobble! Not a clean catch.*

Yes. That's how it was. *Not a clean catch. Pay attention, Maria.* Maria wondered if she'd overestimated her own skills. She could pitch. She could send those balls out sweetly on the uptick of her pendulum arm. But did she have what it took to be on a team?

CHAPTER SIX

The Uncles

EMILIO HAD FALLEN ASLEEP WAITING FOR HER under the tree. Maria had to wake him up when it was time to go. She practically had to carry him at first, but by the time they got to the river he was wide awake and running at full tilt. She wondered if they'd run into the German prisoners someplace. The thought of fugitive prisoners loose in town remained at once exciting and faintly disturbing.

By the time they got home, the house was filling up, but Papi was nowhere. The uncles had come calling; the air buzzed with their talk in Punjabi and English all mixed together. They threw in a little Spanish when they joked with Mamá, swearing she was so beautiful she made all their hearts beat faster. To Maria's relief, Mamá was too busy to interrogate her about why they were late.

The uncles brought food—chicken curry and vegetables. Finally Papi arrived, all hot and sweaty. He kissed Mamá quickly and murmured apologies for his lateness. "I had to go over there," he said.

"It's all right, Kartar," Mamá said. "They're just arriving."

"Where'd you go, Papi?" Maria said. "Over where?"

"Don't bother Papi," said Mamá.

Papi patted Maria's head and then Emilio's as if his thoughts were elsewhere. His hand lingered a moment on Emilio's fuzzy new haircut. A quick shadow passed over his face. Then he went back out to the room adjoining the kitchen, where the men were gathered.

Mamá promptly recruited Maria to help her knead dough. Maria said, "Where did Papi go?"

"To the camp," Mamá said. "Camp Beale."

"Why?"

"We need farmhands," Mamá said, and darted a look at Maria as if to tell her that this much talk was enough and plenty. Maria buttoned her lip and kneaded.

India was where Papi's thoughts usually went when the uncles came—which they sometimes did on weekends, or else they'd gather at church and get a picnic ready while the women and children went to Mass. It was out of the ordinary to have them all come home on a weekday. Something must have happened. Maybe there was news from Punjab, the province in India where Papi came from, a faraway place that he still thought of as home. How could that be? He'd left that place twenty years before on account of being the youngest son. When their father died, Papi was left with no land to farm. It was a mystery how he could still care about such a place, but he did. Just look at how carefully he kept his Indian coins—annas and pice he called them, instead of nickels and dimes—in a little bowl on the mantelpiece. He let the children play with them, but they always had to be put back where they belonged.

In the next room, the conversation rose to a hum. It grew louder, then louder still. Maria could only understand snatches. "Legal . . . land . . . free."

"Germans . . . Angrez . . ." That last meant English—the language, or was it the people, the British? Yes, that was it. The British with their funny way of talking that the WACs had to learn. The British who were America's allies but they ruled India still, even though the Revolution had long ago defeated them here. Here the British were history, but in India they were still in the present.

History was such a complicated thing. *Whose side is the*

right side? Maria thought. And what if the uncles got their way, and the British left India the way they left America? Would the uncles go back? Would Papi?

Suddenly the matter of wearing shorts to practice did not seem very important at all. The world had just expanded to unthinkable proportions—or maybe it was Maria who had shrunk right back into her place.

The uncles laughed a lot, usually. It struck her that they were not laughing now.

Mamá threw the rotis on the griddle, turning them until they puffed up with hot air, then flipping them out onto a platter, folding a little shredded cheese into each one to make a pile of enchiladas with cilantro and chopped tomato tucked inside as flavor surprises. It was adha-adha food, half Mexican, half Punjabi. Halves that fit together to make comfort.

"Here, help me put the food on the table," Mamá said.

The chicken curry was hot. Cauliflower and potatoes steamed in their tomato gravy. Someone had brought a bowl of yogurt, salted and spiced, with grated cucumber mixed into it.

Mamá was reaching for the dish of enchiladas when Emilio clattered in from the front room, his eyes wide.

"What happened to you?" Mamá asked.

Emilio looked up at Mamá in pure shock. "That man in there," he said. "He made Papi cry."

For the first time ever in all her life, Maria saw Mamá shaken. Her hand jerked. The platter tipped, sending folded rotis tumbling all over the counter.

CHAPTER SEVEN

The Man Who Made Papi Cry

"STAY CALM," MAMÁ INSTRUCTED, GATHERING THE rotis up from the counter and replacing the filling as best she could. "Maria, call Papi and the uncles."

Soon the men clustered around the table while Mamá handed out plates. There weren't enough chairs for everyone, but Papi pulled one out for the oldest visitor, a white-haired man with a long beard and a turban on his head. He spoke only Punjabi. The uncles called him Bauji. Maria had seen him somewhere before, had heard his halting voice. But where? It was a long time ago, that was for sure.

Papi's eyes were teary. His face wore a look Maria had never seen before. She could not read the look and she was not used to that.

"He's the one," Emilio whispered, wriggling out from Mamá's reach, his breath hot in Maria's ear.

Mamá grabbed Emilio back and plunked him not too gently on the kitchen counter, setting a plate next to him to discourage more whispering.

Maria tried not to stare at the old man. She helped Mamá serve the food.

The old man would not touch the chicken. He accepted only half a roti and a spoonful of vegetables.

"It's a sad day." Ahmed Khan, Connie's papa, spoke quietly from the kitchen counter, as he filled his plate from Mamá's heaped dishes. "We've lost a friend and brother."

Brother. Papi and the uncles saw each other that way. Who was this lost brother?

"And Bauji has lost his son," said Ahmed Uncle.

"So he won't eat chicken?"

"It's the custom among Sikh people," said Ahmed Uncle. "No meat when you are in mourning."

Maria looked at his plate, with Mamá's chicken curry spilling its fragrance over a mound of rice. "But not you," she said.

He smiled. "I'm Muslim," said Connie's papa. "Or my father is. Was. It's different for us. Well . . ." He came to the table, and sat down as if he was tired. He made as if to take a piece of roti to his mouth, then put it back on his plate. "Muslim, Catholic, Sikh—all the same, only different." He bent over his plate, looking up only to say to Mamá, "Delicious, Hortensia."

Mamá nodded her thanks but said nothing.

Such mysteries were in the air. The old man's dead son, and the ways of all these faiths in the big, wide world. Maria had known for a while that Connie's father and Papi believed in different religions, but just what that meant, she was still not sure.

Bauji set his plate down. The gesture caught Maria's eye, and something else as well: the slope of a nose, maybe, or the curve of a cheekbone and suddenly it all made sense. *We've lost a brother. Bauji has lost his son.*

She knew where she'd seen this bearded man before. At the Stockton temple. That same temple where Papi's old prayer book came from. The temple where they went every year on the birthday of Guru Nanak, the holy man who had founded Papi's Sikh religion hundreds of years ago.

The temple was a clear, sharp memory for Maria, with its wide, flat steps and great hall filled with old bearded men who made fiery speeches in Punjabi. The temple was song and drum and the accordion-like bellow of the harmonium. It was rich, sweet kara-parshad, full to bursting with butter, flour, and sugar and stirred (this was the exciting part that always made Emilio shriek with awe and delight) with the small, sharp sword that Papi called a kirpan. Stirred and served in dollops right into your cupped hands so you gobbled it up really fast and let its last grainy crumbs melt into bliss in your mouth.

Maria didn't understand the speeches she heard at the temple, but they stirred her blood as if the words themselves were swords, making her feel part of something big and important.

And now she knew. She hadn't recognized him. He looked so very old and stricken. "You're Janie's grandpa!" she cried. This time no one told her to be quiet.

The old man looked at her with kind and faded eyes. No fire in them now.

Which meant—which meant—the lines connected in her mind.

Gian Gill, Ahmed Khan, and Papi had come together from India to Panama, then north through Mexico and into California. Papi was the oldest of the three, Gian the youngest. *My brothers,* Papi always said. *My brothers.*

They had all worked on the Sacramento Northern Railroad together, had starved and celebrated together, endured and lost and won together. In Imperial Valley they had dug ditches and canals and made the dry land flower. They had married their Mexican wives within weeks of each other, become godfathers to each other's children.

Now Gian Gill, Janie's papa, would not be coming home.

This has not happened to me in my life until now, Maria thought. For the first time ever, someone I know has died. On the heels of which, another thought. *Poor Janie.* If . . . when . . . the war ended, others would come home, but there would be no parties to welcome Gian Uncle. Only a hole in the place where he used to live and work and be.

The old man stood, murmured words of thanks in Punjabi to Mamá, to which she replied in Spanish, neither of them seeming to feel the need for translation. Then everyone went back to the front room, even Maria and Emilio. They sat on the floor as Bauji brought out a book and mumbled a Punjabi prayer in his fractured old man voice. Slowly, slowly, many of the men joined in, ending with a call and reply that fell on Maria's ears with a small jolt of recognition.

From the family's once-a-year visit to the Stockton

temple, she knew what this meant because she had asked and Papi had explained that many prayers ended in this way:

Waheguruji ki khalsa.

Waheguruji ki fateh.

Bole so nihaal

Sat sri akaal.

It was about victory—victory to those who followed the teachings of the Guru. Ahmed Uncle and a few of the other Muslim men sat in silence. They did not join in, but they bowed their heads. They clasped their hands respectfully together.

"Papi, what happened? Who died? Why? When? Why were you crying?"

Papi gave Mamá a worried look. "Bauji has lived through many battles," Papi said, "and now this war has taken his son."

"Battles?" Emilio's eyes lit up. "With guns, Papi?"

"Aho." Papi nodded. "But I think he's done fighting now."

"Was he in Germany?" Maria asked. Bauji was too old to fight in this war, right? Some other war, it must have been. The last one.

Papi shook his head. "Nahin-nahin."

"Japan?"

"No, Son. The freedom struggle."

Freedom. That could only mean India's freedom. "From the—" Maria tried the word on for size. "Angrez?" The word that the Punjabi men used for the English who ruled India.

"Aho," Papi said. "From the Angrez." He rumpled her hair, but he looked as if his mind was somewhere else.

Mamá's lips pursed, as they always did when Papi talked about India and freedom and the British. "It's hard enough," she murmured, but said no more.

Maria knew the end of that murmur. She'd heard it before. Hard enough to live your life working from morning till night. Hard enough to make do, to pay the bills. Hard enough to be a foreigner in America. Why get mixed up in these other political things? Mamá herself was from another country, yet she didn't worry daily about the politics of Mexico. How long could you hold a faraway land so close to your heart? But now, loyal to Papi, Mamá said none of those things.

"Did Bauji kill anyone?" Emilio wanted to know.

"Such talk," said Mamá. "Of course he didn't."

But from the look on Papi's face, Maria wondered if he had.

CHAPTER EIGHT

Americans, All

BALL PRACTICE THE FOLLOWING DAY WAS A WHIRL of fumbles and drops for Maria. The more she tried, the less she could pay attention. Maybe it was yesterday evening's news, still spinning around in her mind. Maybe it was because other things lay heavily on her. Ball practice itself. The time she was spending here every day after school, without telling Mamá and Papi.

Janie wasn't there. No one expected her to show up, naturally, and there was much whispering about her dad. Even Miss Newman said something about "our sad news" and held a moment of silence for "the lost heroes of the war," which seemed like a strangely grand thing to call somebody's papa.

Then there was the small, selfish matter of suitable

clothes, which hers were not. And worst of all, where was Emilio? She'd told him to wait for her. He'd promised. So where was he? All of which led to Maria pitching wildly and striking out when she was up to bat.

When she got home afterward, she was all out of breath from hurrying. She'd gotten a ride part of the way with Connie and her dad. They'd dropped her off just past the bridge and she had run all the way from there.

Mamá and Emilio were sitting at the kitchen table, Emilio with a droop to his shoulders, no laughter in his body, his face red, his hair all tousled, and scratches on his cheek. He wouldn't even look at Maria.

Mamá, on the other hand, pinned Maria with a glare that stalled her right there in the middle of the kitchen floor.

"Look what happened," Mamá said.

"What?" Maria's guilt rose up inside her and burned all over her face. "Nothing. Nothing's happened."

"To your brother," Mama said. "You'd know if you had walked home with him." She pursed her lips at Emilio. "Tell her."

Emilio sucked his cheeks in. He twisted and turned about. When it became clear that a rock could have learned about patience from Mamá, he finally said, all in one breath, "They teased me. And I wasn't gonna tell Mamá, but I had to, Maria, and will you still give me half of your tin cans?"

Oh. No. He was mad for the war-effort armbands that kids could get for turning in the masses of flattened tin cans they hauled to town every few months. Now she couldn't say a thing to shush him up and anyway, she could see from Mamá's face that she knew everything.

Emilio fiddled with the end of his shirt. He tapped his feet on the kitchen stool as if, given the chance, he'd bolt right out of the room. He said, "They bet I didn't know how many stars in the flag."

"Go on." Mamá leaned forward.

"'Cos I'm a foreigner," Emilio said. "That's what they said—Joey and Charley. 'Half and half,' they said, that's what we are. I said, 'There's forty-eight, so there. That means I'm not.'"

And Mamá was silent.

Emilio burst out. "Mami, I am American—no?"

Mamá wiped her floury hands on her apron. "M'ijo, you can't get in fights. It helps nobody, and it only hurts you." She got up, walked around the table. She lifted his shirt. "Look at you."

Maria breathed in sharp and quick at the bruise underneath turning purple. "Oh, 'Milio."

"I hit them," said Emilio fiercely. "Then they tried to catch me. I would have gotten away, but I fell."

Mamá put both hands on Emilio's shoulders and she said to Maria, "You have something to say?"

"I didn't know . . ." Maria said.

Emilio said, "Mamá, they say bad things about Papi and you."

Maria almost quit breathing.

Mamá got all sharp then, her dark brown eyes growing shiny hard. "What do they say?" Her voice skimmed a knife edge.

Emilio took a big breath. "They say that Papi can't own his own farm because—" His face crumpled.

"Tell me," said Mamá softly.

He breathed the words all in a rush. "I told them it's all lies, what they say."

"What is all lies?" Her voice was so quiet you'd never know she was getting angry, but Maria knew. There were lines that showed up on Mamá's forehead only when she was about ready to spit fire.

Emilio said, "They say in California we don't want

Hindus to own land. We drove the Japs out and now it's your—our— It's lies, Mamá! It's not our turn!"

Hindus? Japs? Those words that so many used as careless insults fell on Maria's ears like blows. Our turn? "Mamá?" Maria couldn't believe it. "Is this true?" The Japanese were all gone, she knew that, to some faraway place in the desert—taken for their own safety, everyone said, but no one ever talked about why that was so. Sally Yamate from her class was gone, and Eddie and Sam and the Ebiharas and more. All gone, and for so long now she could barely remember their faces. They were Americans, all, weren't they? Why had she not even thought about that before?

Mamá would not look at either Maria or Emilio. She straightened up and leaned against the counter. The anger lines went away, but Mamá sighed like the air going out of dough. "It's not lies," she said at last. "It's true."

"What?" Maria felt the words hit with small jolts.

Mamá told them about the law, and it was plain cruel. No one from the whole big land of Asia could buy farms or houses anywhere in California.

And it was worse. People like Papi could not become citizens. At one time it was Chinese and Indians who couldn't. Now the Chinese were allowed, because they had become allies during the war. But Indians were not.

"They are trying," said Mamá. "They have even sent letters to Congress. But I don't know who's listening."

How could any of this be true?

"Go take off that shirt and put on a clean one," said Mamá to Emilio. "The skin's not broken. No llores."

Emilio listened and didn't cry. He went upstairs without another word. Mamá's eyes followed him.

Maria got ready to disappear too. Mamá said without turning her head, "You! Don't move."

Sigh. Maria stopped. Mamá looked right at her now. "When times are tough, family is all we got."

Maria nodded.

"So you tell me, how come you're sneaking around behind our backs?"

"Mamá!" Maria protested. "I tried to tell Papi. You know I tried. First he said no ball playing because no shorts. Then he said maybe he'll talk to Connie's papa. But then— nothing! Nothing, Mamá! I've been waiting and waiting."

Mamá said, "He's got a lot to worry about. You know that. These are little things, when he's got so much."

"It's not a little thing to me," Maria said.

Mamá said, "Life is sometimes unfair, and you children have to understand that."

"It's not my fault about the laws and the boys saying mean things to . . ." But she stopped, because Mamá raised an eyebrow at her. Maria had to blink back her anger and regret. She hadn't been there to stop those boys. That was her fault, not being there. Sometimes it wasn't just what you did that counted against you. It was what you didn't do.

Mamá said, "When countries go to war, people start thinking enemies are everywhere. So we're hearing ugly talk, and now this fighting. You keep an eye on Emilio— you're his big sister, you gotta help him out. That's all I'm telling you."

"What about me?" Maria said. "Don't I count?"

Mamá drew a long, deep breath. She said, "You count. But Emilio can't walk home by himself."

"And if I make sure he doesn't, then I can play?"

"I'll talk to Papi," Mamá said.

"He's so stubborn!" Maria cried.

"Don't you talk like that about your papi." Mamá sniffed. Then she looked at Maria sideways and added, "Stubborn? I know someone who got that from him."

CHAPTER NINE

Papi's Story

"ANYBODY'S GOING TO TALK TO PAPI ABOUT WHAT happened, it's going to be me," Mamá said to Maria and Emilio, and there was enough steel in her voice that they both nodded wordlessly. Maria waited for Papi to come home. Then she went up to her room, which was not so much a room as a stack of mattresses on the landing next to the steamer trunk. She decided to listen at the door to their bedroom in case Mamá was ready to do her talking. She crept up to the door, put her ear to it. But she didn't hear anything relevant, only a lot of back-and-forthing about responsibility and doing the right thing.

Wham! The door opened. Maria practically toppled over.

"¿Qué pasa?" Mamá bent down low as if she was trying

to see what Maria might possibly have been examining so closely in the knotted wood.

"Ants," said Maria desperately.

"All lies," said Mamá.

That night over dinner, Mamá once again said nothing. Nothing. It was as if Emilio's fight with the Hamilton boys had never happened, nor Mamá's conversation with Maria about softball.

Over dinner, Mamá was all sugar and smiles. "How about one of your stories, Kartar?" she prompted over frijoles and rice. "Been a long time since you told one of them."

"Papi, tell about when you came to America!" Emilio loved that story, knew its every turn.

"I had heard," Papi began on cue, "about a big canal, and rumors they were going to build more locks and dams and needed workmen."

Emilio's mouth opened in a little pink O. He is a baby still, Maria thought with a sudden pang. Tall and growing, maybe, but inside himself, he is small. He is six. It is easy to hurt him.

I, she thought, am tougher. Knowing things does that to you.

"But by the time I got to this land of Panama," Papi was saying, "they did not need more workmen."

"So you walked to California!" cried Emilio, his frown melting like ice on a summer day. "And you walked and you walked!"

Mamá murmured, "Through Mexico. That is a lot of walking." It was a refrain grown from habit, this story having been told plenty of times over the years.

Papi winked at Mamá. "I walked, and walked, and it got very hot. My turban protected me from the sun. But people were afraid of me, because I looked so different." He touched his head as if those traditional folds of cloth were still there. "So I took it off. I folded it and put it in my bag. That was a big mistake."

A pause. Emilio whispered, "Go on, Papi."

"And I kept on walking all the way to California."

Emilio chuckled, gearing up for the ending. Maria sighed. She had listened in delight to every turn of that story, many, many times before. Why did it suddenly taste stale?

"By the time I got there, the sun was so hot, it burned the hair right off my head. It never grew back so long again."

Emilio roared with laughter. "It's a joke!" he cried.

"You cut your hair so they'd give you a job in America."

"People didn't understand," Papi said. "They wouldn't hire someone so foreign like me, with a turban on my head."

Why in the world had Maria ever thought that story was funny? She could see now it was sad, desperately sad. How come she'd never noticed that before? So bitter, the reality that lurked underneath the laughter. She wanted Papi to stop, stop it now, stop pretending that there was anything amusing about that journey of his.

What is wrong with me? she thought. *Why can't I just laugh along? Why is this story now sticking in my throat?*

"Papi, you're not foreign," said Emilio.

Mamá gave him a warning look, a look that said, *Don't say any more. Nada.* Then she said, "Maria, get the chabacanos." Mamá's magic hand had turned last year's dried apricots into a cobbler with milk and a generous portion of the month's sugar ration. Enough to distract Emilio.

"What for?" Papi said in surprise. "What are we celebrating?"

"Nothing," said Mamá. Then she said, "Us. Can't we just celebrate because there is us?"

They looked at each other as if neither had ever seen

such a fine sight before. Maria felt like a traitor for harboring small, mean resentments in her small, mean mind.

Later that night, after everyone had gone to sleep, Maria crept back down to the kitchen and talked it out with Guadalupe, the Lady herself. Mary, whose tears mattered. Mary, who prayed for the living, and over her the angels watched . . . .

"La Lupe," said Maria to her namesake, "Can't you make the world a better place?" And just so the Sikh holy teachers didn't feel left out, she laid a hand on Papi's yellow prayer book and said, "You also." She murmured those words from Bauji's prayer—Bole so nihaal, sat sri akaal.

Then, just to be sure, Maria went on to label a few world-changing requests personally.

Change the laws.

Change Papi so he listens.

That is not too selfish a wish. Is it?

Mary Mother of God smiled her patient plaster smile at Maria who was named for her.

For Emilio's sake, justice demanded that those mean boys be flattened into the dust, but Maria had a feeling that wasn't the type of wish upon which the saints would look kindly.

CHAPTER TEN

Home and Kitchen

THE BRIGHT POSTCARD FROM TÍA MANUELA STOOD propped against the old RCA radio. Its colors glowed against the dark wood veneer of the cabinet.

It was only the fourth day of practice, and Maria was missing it. She'd intended to go, but Emilio's fight and Mamá's words had worked on her mind all day, and at the last minute, she'd chickened out. She'd walked home with Emilio after school like a good sister. Being sisterly should have made her feel good, but it didn't. Every step, the whole way home, she wished she'd stayed for practice instead.

But now she held the postcard in her hand. How fine it looked with its views of all those places in Southern California—Lake Arrowhead, the round dome of the Palomar Observatory, Mission San Juan Capistrano with the swallows flying around the dome, Newport Bay, and the peace bridge on Mount Rubidoux. The postcard's linen grain glowed in sun-drenched colors. It lifted Maria's spirits just the way Tía herself did.

On the back, Tía Manuela had written in her customary round hand:

I hope you're all well.

Be strong.

Love you and miss you.

   Manuela.

The postcard, the message, the feel of it in her hand. All of it made Maria feel as if a rainbow had splashed up unexpectedly into a drab sky. *I hope you're all well.* That was for everyone in the family, of course. But the next words—*Be strong*—sent a little tingle through Maria. Tía knew her niece's heart, and Maria knew that those words were especially for her. She decided to be strong at that very moment. "Mamá," Maria said to her mother, who was working at her sewing machine, "did you ever talk to Papi?"

"About what?" said Mamá.

"Playing ball. If I make sure I walk home with Emilio."

"Oh, that," Mamá said. "Yes."

"And?" Yes. That was all? What did that mean, yes? Yes, she had talked to him? And so . . . ?

"And then what?" Maria burst out. "What did you say? What did he say? Can I play?"

Mamá gave Maria the kind of look that discouraged further outbursts. "You can play," she said. "But you will make sure that Emilio stays until you are done and then you will walk home together. ¿Comprende?"

"Sí, Mamá. And what about getting shorts?"

"Oh." Mamá squinted at the needle on the old Singer sewing machine as she worked the thread through its tiny eye. "That I didn't ask. One thing at a time." She held the edges of fabric in place and cranked the handle of the machine, ratcheting a tidy row of stitches into the skirt hem. Once she was done with a pile of them, Papi would take the dresses into town and drop them off to Doña Elena's tailoring shop on the corner of Plumas and Forbes. Papi sometimes said, *Hortensia, one day I'll be a rich man and you won't need to take in sewing anymore.* Mamá always shook her head as if that would be the day.

"I need to get shorts, or a short skirt. I could play in

long pants even. If that's okay with Papi. Just not in a long skirt, Mamá."

"Hmm," Mamá said, inspecting the hem. "Let's see, m'ija."

"I'll ask Papi," Maria said. "If he says okay, will you make me some?"

Mamá said, "You're old enough you can make your own. I'll show you if you like, if you'll sit still long enough." Doña Elena paid Mamá twenty cents a hem, so Mamá was grudging about using her sewing time for anything else.

Maria sat up straight. "I will, Mamá, I will. I promise." Possibility was the most wonderful thing. It sent a shiver coursing through her. "Oh, Mamá, I hope Papi says yes."

Mamá said, "I don't know, Maria."

"But Mamá —"

"The new workmen came today. Papi's out with the picking trucks. No telling when he's coming back. It's a tough time, okay? So—we'll see."

So much for being strong. How could she be strong if nobody had the time to listen to her? *Stop it, Maria,* she told herself. *He said you could play.* That was good enough for now. It had to be. Maria clicked the radio on.

"Don't lose my radio station," said Mamá.

Mamá claimed that *Ozzie and Harriet* helped her practice her English, but Maria suspected she really liked the show because it made her laugh. "No, Mamá." Maria twiddled the tuning knob. "I'll switch it back for you, okay?"

"Okay."

Maria turned the volume up. "America's young men are off fighting for our country," said the voice from KMYC, the Marysville station, punctuated by crackles.

"What are you listening to?" asked Emilio.

"They are dreaming of the girls they left behind." The radio's magic cat's eye spun blue and green as the crackles settled into audible words. "But here at home, the girls are playing ball."

"Shh," Maria said. "They're talking about the girls' league."

"Here is a message to young ladies from Arthur Meyerhoff, owner of the All-American Girls Professional Baseball League."

A message to young ladies. All-American girls. Clear to static and back again, crackles and all, the words fell like music upon Maria's ear.

"Patriotic fans are ensuring a bright future for our girls in the ball field," said the league owner, "with teams like the Racine Belles and the Rockford Peaches, the Millerettes and the Grand Rapids Chicks. Families are turning out at the ballparks to see them play. Let me tell you, my friends, the girls on those teams are patriots. Many have husbands, sweethearts, brothers, and relatives overseas. They play for them as much as for their fans. You young girls listening out there—and we know some of you are playing ball in your communities—well, rest assured that one day you too can display your abilities not only in the home and kitchen but also . . ."

The radio connection sputtered into a storm of static, but Maria knew what those last words were.

"On the ball field!" she yelled, unable to stop herself.

"¡Ay, Dios mío!" Mamá said. "Don't make my heart jump like that."

When Papi came home, Maria knew at once that something was wrong. He took his fedora off and put it on the hook behind the door. He rolled up his sleeves, and the steel bangle that he always wore clanged against the knob as he closed the door behind him. He would not look at anyone. He handed Maria a bag of greens to put away, discards from the day's picking. He didn't pull Mamá aside to talk as he usually did when there were grown-up things to discuss. He just sat down at the table and put his head in his hands.

Maria knew better than to raise the question of clothes for ball practice.

Mamá tried to talk Papi into a better mood. "Did it go well with the workmen, Kartar?"

"Well enough," Papi said. "They are extra hands. They will do."

"Are they German?" Maria asked.

"Aho," said Papi. "They speak a little English. No Español."

"They're bad guys, Papi!" Emilio exclaimed. He was over his trauma of the day before, tucking with relish into warm tortillas and the chicken curry with its few pieces of meat that Mamá doled out in strict rations for everyone.

Papi sighed. "Bad guys, good guys . . . they are farmhands. Willing to dig the ditches and clear the weeds."

"They have no choice," Mamá said. "They are prisoners, so they must do as they are told."

"There is no one else," said Papi. "I have no choice either."

Neither do I, Maria's evil voice said in her mind. *I am not allowed to do the things I want to do, and instead I must do as I am told. Being a kid is like being a prisoner, but that does not make me bad, does it?*

"Any news about those two who got away?" Mamá asked.

"Sheriff's deputies are out looking," Papi said. "And the

military police too." The county sheriff had posted wanted notices in town, and the posse was out on the highway.

"They're dangerous, Papi," Emilio said.

"Who says?" said Mamá.

"Everybody!"

"Everybody should mind their business," said Mamá. "Eat your frijoles."

Maria ate her frijoles. She ate every last crumb on her plate just as she knew Mamá always wanted them to. "Papi," she said. "Thank you."

"For what, kuriye?" The Punjabi word for daughter came automatically to him.

"Mamá told me. You said I could play softball." Her heart just about brimmed over.

"Oh." Papi waved his hand. "You go play, go play." But honest to God, he looked as if he couldn't even remember having given that permission.

Against her better judgment, Maria forged on. "I need clothes, Papi. To wear for practice."

Mamá shook her head and sighed.

Maria kept going. "Okay? I can't—"

But Papi interrupted her. Maybe he hadn't even heard her. He said, rubbing a spot on his chin where he'd nicked himself shaving that morning, "Becker's going to sell the orchards."

"What?" said Mamá.

Maria's plea for shorts dried up midsentence. Emilio's mouth fell open.

"He's going to sell our lease," Papi said. "Maybe move to Sacramento, he thinks. We can stay until it's sold."

The clock ticked through their silence. Even Emilio hushed.

"He thinks maybe soon," said Papi, answering the question that no one could ask. He stood up, pushing his chair back with a creak.

Stay? Until it's sold? Soon? How soon? And then what? But Mamá's glance of warning told Maria clear as clear that she could not ask these or any other questions. Not now.

"That man," Mamá said. "What would his wife say, God rest her soul?"

Papi paced the room as if he were seeing it for the first time. He adjusted a picture on the wall, even though it seemed quite straight already. It had always hung there, Mamá and Papi's wedding picture. Papi standing proud and straight in his dark suit, eyes looking right into the camera. His face unsmiling but with a light in his eyes. Mamá beside him in a white embroidered dress, her veil held with pearls over her curly hair, her pointy white shoes elegant and perfect on their slight heels, a bouquet held lightly in one gloved hand.

Papi turned from the picture and looked around the room, and he was a different man. There was a hardness in his eyes that Maria had never seen before.

CHAPTER ELEVEN

Not Ever Again

"YOU CAN'T WALK HOME ALONE," MARIA TOLD EMILIO, "so you have to wait till I'm done playing ball."

"Does Mamá know?"

"Of course she knows," Maria told him. She ended up pledging to feed the chickens the next morning, in exchange for his promise that he'd stay put.

As Miss Newman chose infield players, Maria looked over to make sure Emilio wasn't roughhousing with the bigger boys—what were those boys doing, anyway, still hanging around? She was relieved to see her brother on his tummy in the shade of a walnut tree, busy scratching in the dirt with a stick.

"Lucy, you're the pitcher," Miss Newman said. "You—to first base—and you . . . you . . . you to second base, third base, shortstop." Dot, Connie, Maria. "Sal and Milly, right field, center . . . and where's Elizabeth?"

Someone said she hadn't been in school today. Something about going to Sharp Park. Maria was not sure where that was. Elizabeth's dad was always doing business trips all over the state, Maria knew, but why did she have to go?

Miss Newman's attention shifted. She looked over their shoulders. Her voice grew soft. "Janie?" she said.

They all turned. Janie had come up unnoticed. She stood at the rough patch that served as home base, and her face had an odd, frozen look. She said nothing.

"I am so sorry," Miss Newman said. "I heard the news."

Everyone was gathered around Janie by now. Her mouth trembled, but she still said nothing.

"It's good to see you, Janie," Miss Newman said.

"Thank you," Janie mumbled, not catching anyone's eye. She was like a machine with broken springs, as if the news about her father had taken everything apart.

"Oh, Janie!" Maria cried.

"Easy, Maria," Connie warned.

But Maria rushed to Janie's side, something inside her giving. She meant to hug Janie. That was all. Just a hug from a friend. Only Janie blocked the hug with her arm. Blocked it, and worse, she pushed Maria away. "Don't," she said between clenched teeth. "Just. Don't. Okay?"

Maria backed off.

"Leave her alone," Connie said. "She's still in shock."

"Fine," said Maria, and it came out sounding not fine at all, it came out sounding angry. Which maybe it was, deep down inside, a small wisp of hurt licking awake. The heat rose flaming to Maria's face.

"Don't get in a sweat," Connie said.

"What do you mean?" Maria protested. "I only said—"

"I need another player," said Miss Newman hurriedly. "Janie—left field. Okay?"

Janie moved to where Miss Newman pointed. Outside the fence that bordered the outfield, the boys had begun to chase each other around a tree.

As the girls shuffled to their places, Connie was still bristling. It was Connie's way. No one was as good and loyal a friend as Connie, but when she felt strongly about something, she could really sink her teeth into it. "Her papa could have gotten a farmer's deferment," she said in a low voice. "But he didn't."

Miss Newman was giving some other instructions,

and for some reason the boys were jumping the fence and joining them, but now Connie was deep into her verbal tug-of-war with Maria.

"A lot of men got that kind of deferment," Connie said. "Your papa did, right, so he didn't have to go off and fight?"

"Maybe he did," Maria said, "but so what? Your dad didn't go either, did he?"

"How can you say that?" said Connie, irate.

"What? How can I say what?"

"Girls," Miss Newman prompted. "Ready?"

"My dad's got a game leg." Connie's face was red. Her finger was jabbing the air in front of Maria's nose. "You know that. From the polio when he was a kid. They wouldn't take him, all right? They won't take a man with a limp in the military."

Maria's heart plummeted practically down to her shoes. She knew that. She knew that Ahmed Uncle walked with a limp. What was she thinking, lashing out at Connie like that?

"He tried," Connie said in a strangled voice. "He wanted to go, okay? He wanted to go."

And then she turned her face away from Maria as if she could no longer bear to look at her. And truth to tell, Maria did not want to look back. Because what did that mean, exactly, that Papi had gotten that farm deferment? Did it mean that he was too cowardly to go fight?

"Connie, Maria!" Miss Newman blew a quick burst on her whistle.

"Sorry," Maria muttered. The air in the dirt field, which had seemed perfectly breathable a minute ago, suddenly seemed to rise up and suffocate her. The boys were lining up to bat. To bat! Miss Newman, it seemed, had invited them to come along and help the girls get their skills up. Emilio was perched on the fence, his eyes wide, watching this new development.

He'd better stay put, Maria thought distractedly, only she couldn't pay attention to him now.

Shortstop, she said to herself. I'm *shortstop*. She tried to focus on the pitching and batting. She let her inner announcer voice swing into place in her mind and it did, it did.

Mondo hits the ball to Connie. She misses, it goes right through her legs. Second ball fielded cleanly, thrown back to the catcher, and it's going to be me next, it's me, eye on the ball, eye—on—the—ball.

But there was Janie all stiff and cold, and Connie's

anger still alive between them. Maria got down into a ready crouch, tried to concentrate. "Ready, Lucy?" called Miss Newman.

Oh, I am so thoughtless, so stupid, Maria said to herself.

Swish! Lucy's ball flew out. Mondo Khan swung his bat.

Glove down and ready. Maria bent her knees, bent them the way she was supposed to. Glove hand down and—yes, yes, yes—she had her eye on the ball.

Smack! The bat connected.

Low to the ground.

Eye on the ball.

But the ball flew to her left. Too low. Maria overreached, missed, and thudded to the ground, her elbow grinding painfully into the dirt. Her skirt rode high. She groaned. It wasn't just her arm. She was going to have a beauty of a bruise on her leg as well.

"Help, murder, police!" a voice cried out. Tim Singh's voice, from the batting lineup.

A chorus replied, "Maria fell in the grease!" And was that Emilio from his perch on the fence—it couldn't be, could it?—joining the boys in their guffaws?

"Help, murder, police!

Maria fell in the grease.

We laughed so hard—

We fell in the lard!"

Miss Newman blew her whistle and blew it and blew it to silence the boys' hooting and hollering. The mocking playground song died down as Maria lay in the dust for what felt like an eternity. You could add anyone's name to that song. Most often these days it was Hitler or Mussolini. Today, it was her.

Maria picked herself up. Blinded by tears that came welling out of her fury—at herself, the boys, Emilio, Janie, the war, Connie, the world purely full of unfairness—she ran.

She thought she heard Connie calling, "Wait, Maria!" but it couldn't have been, because Connie wasn't going to be speaking to her, possibly not ever again.

She ran, not caring where, forgetting all about Emilio, just trying to get as far as she could from the laughter ringing in her ears. Not even Miss Newman crying out, "Maria, stop! Listen!" could make her turn back.

Maria didn't quit running until the echoes of the voices from the playing field behind her died down in her head. It was only when she stopped at last that she saw where she was. Right smack dab in the middle of Mr. Becker's rows of peach trees.

Becker! The oso. Elizabeth's daddy, owner of the land where Papi worked his lease. The man who people said would just as soon shoot at you as speak to you. Heart thudding, she turned around to get out of there. Fast. Papi would have a fit if he knew she'd been running around in the orchard. The children were allowed to pick fruit off the trees by the house, but that was all. The orchard was off limits.

She was almost to the fence when she heard a voice. "Hey! Who's that? Stop!"

Maria halted in her tracks even while her mind screamed silently at her, Run, run, run!

Steps crunched behind her through the dry grass. Maria turned.

"Oh, it's you," said Mr. Becker. "What're you doing here? Your old man send you with a message or something?"

"No," Maria muttered.

"What's that? Speak up, girl!"

Maria swallowed. Please, she prayed to the god of Santa Rosa and Papi's god of his book and any other god who might be *listening, let me just get away from him.*

"No, sir," she said, and her trembling nearly smothered the words. She turned to go.

"Not so fast," said Becker. "So what are you doing here, then?" He peered at her. "Helping yourself to free peaches?"

"No!" said Maria, outraged.

"You sure?"

"Yes."

"Empty out your pockets," Mr. Becker commanded.

What? It took Maria a second to understand what he meant. What he expected to find, stolen off his precious trees. As if she would do such a thing.

"I didn't take any!" she protested.

"Pockets. Come on." He came closer, smelling of sweat and horses.

For a moment she thought again of running. She could probably outrun him, but what was the use? Running would equal guilt. He'd only be certain she'd come for those peaches.

She turned her pocket out, letting fall a feather and a torn handkerchief and a broken pencil. The other pocket. Out fell the stub of a ticket from last month's showing of *The Three Caballeros* that Papi had taken them to see at Smith's Theatre.

Maria made herself look up at Arnold Becker and hold that look right there. How pale his eyes are, she thought. *He has eyes like glass, and if there is even a shred of a feeling swimming around behind them, wouldn't I see it now?* She almost felt sorry for Elizabeth. Imagine having this man for a daddy. Maybe it was true, the things people said about him. That he had a rack of guns in his kitchen, had used them to kill people and would do so again.

In the end, Mr. Becker was the one who looked away. "Get on home," he growled.

Maria needed no more prompts. She took off as if the old oso had grown fur and claws right there. She ran until she was in a proper sweat, and it wasn't until she got to the front door that she remembered she'd left Emilio sitting on the fence on Plumas Street, laughing at her.

CHAPTER TWELVE

Trust

MARIA SLUNK INTO THE HOUSE, TO FIND THAT Emilio had made it home by himself.

"I looked for you," he complained, "but you ran off."

"I know. I'm sorry."

But his mouth turned down at the corners and she knew that sorry was just a word. It didn't mend the hurt. He'd waited. He'd kept his word, and she, all caught up in her own hurt feelings, had run away.

Mamá was furious. "You promised me. And I promised Papi that you would not let this child come home on his own. You gonna tell me what happened?"

"Mamá, I fell down. Everyone laughed at me."

"So you ran away?" Mamá said. She made it sound like a completely despicable thing to do.

"I wasn't thinking." A useless excuse, but there it was. The truth.

"That's the problem," Mamá said. "You don't stop to think. Ever. You just say and do the first thing that comes into your head."

"I don't. That's not fair." But she had, hadn't she? She had just done exactly that, more than once.

Mamá was right. That was how Maria was.

"I trusted you," said Mamá.

Guilt rose in Maria, a surging, gushing torrent of it. She pushed it down, down, down, before it drowned her. It was all very well for Mamá to scold, but Mamá didn't know how it felt to be laughed at like that.

"You know that I'm worried about Emilio."

Perhaps it was that rising tide of guilt that made Maria dare to round upon her mother. "You're always worried about Emilio," she cried. "What about me?"

"You watch it," said Mamá.

But Maria couldn't watch it. She was past watching it. "You don't care for me even a bit. I wish I was born into some other family!"

Mamá's eyes flashed fire.

"You have a wicked tongue," she said. "I thought I could trust you. Now I see I was mistaken."

Maria slunk away from those burning eyes. Mamá could see clear into her, all right, but she wasn't going to give Maria one jot of sympathy.

Maria ran upstairs, her heart thumping as if it would burst. She slumped to the floor on the wide landing that was her room, against the old steamer trunk. Its latch dug into her back. She wished she could just slip through the floorboards. She wished she could disappear and never return. She wished . . . no, she could not. She was empty of wishes.

Silence from the kitchen turned into a thunder of knife upon cutting board, Mamá dealing with carrots and beans as if they were her own personal enemy and she their executioner.

Thunk! Thump! Slam! Then click-chop-click! As the cutting sounds slowed, grew more regular, the tide inside Maria ebbed too. On an impulse, she jiggled the latch of the old steamer trunk. Mamá had found it at a sale and brought it home to store old things that didn't fit anywhere else.

Inside were layers of fabric, some old lace shawls, and Emilio's baby blanket. Beneath all that were several flattened sheets of paper, their edges curling with age. Under them, two folded lengths of faded cloth. These Maria extracted with a little shiver of discovery.

She opened up the first, soft and pliable and orangey brown. It was bright on the inside; the color had only faded in patches on top and on the folds. Papi's turbans! Hidden between them was a small comb. A kangha, Papi called it. A memory came ricocheting back to Maria from years ago, when she had been as small as Emilio. No, before Emilio was even born. It was of Papi laughing and showing her how to tie one of these turbans with the hair combed and knotted inside. He'd shown Maria how to wrap the length of fabric and tuck it the way he used to do, before he cut his hair.

And what was this? From the folds of the second turban, a royal blue whose brilliance still shone through between cloudier faded patches, fell a picture. It was of Papi as a young man, before he came to America.

It showed him in some kind of uniform, with a shiny leather strap that ran from his shoulder down to his middle and looped over a belt that circled his waist. He held a stout stick before him. Looking at the grainy gray image, Maria wondered what color the uniform was. It had stripes on the pocket. Were they red and green and gold, or royal blue like the turban?

Look at his face. It was a face you could trust. Unlike Maria, with her heedless tongue.

CHAPTER THIRTEEN

Cash for Your Trash

PLAYING BALL. SUCH A SIMPLE THING FOR A GIRL to want. Yet somewhere along the way it had become filled with guilt and lies and injured pride. On Saturday morning, Maria had to get up early to feed the chickens so she could pay off her debt to Emilio. At least she didn't have to wrangle with her conscience about going to softball practice. For the time being, she decided to leave it alone. She said nothing to Mamá or Papi about softball or shorts or anything. She managed to snatch a few minutes at the radio after Mamá was done listening to Ozzie and Harriet.

The Armed Forces Radio made Maria snap to attention with one sports news item. "Olive Little is a star pitcher for Rockford, winning twenty-one games in the league's first year and pitching the league's first no-hitter that same year in a nine-inning game." Olive Little was a star everybody loved. She turned cartwheels on the field. She made everyone laugh with her flashing smile. A no-hitter! The radio lit a hopeful flame in Maria.

On Saturday too, the little farmhouse rattled and clanged in honor of the war effort. "Take the tin cans to the collection center," Mamá said. "And take the strained grease to the Safeway." She checked the jar on the meat safe. "Yes, that one. There's enough."

"What about the old pots and pans?"

Mamá looked in the corner shelves of the kitchen that served as pantry and storage space. "Those three. Take those."

"Okay," Maria said.

"Stop at the Khans' place," Mamá said.

"Oh, Mamá!" Maria said.

"What? Carmen said she has some things to send along, so you be helpful." They were fast friends, Connie's mother and Mamá. "What's the problem?"

Normally, stopping at the Khan place would have been easy. But not on this day. "Do I have to?" It came out all whiny, which was not what Maria had intended.

"What's the matter? You girls have a quarrel or something?"

"Yeah. Something like that. It's just . . . oh Mamá, she hates me. I was mean to her and now she hates me."

"Was she mean to you first?" Mamá demanded.

Maria had to confess. No, Connie had not been mean first. She, Maria, had been. It was true.

"So then go," said Mamá. "There's no excuse, is there?"

It seemed so plain when she said it that way. Who started the meanness? Who did? She, Maria, that's who. So there was not any excuse, was there? There was not. Maria hung her head.

"Go and make up," said Mamá, still making it all seem ridiculously easy. "But mind you come back right away. There's laundry waiting to do."

A great generous surge of hope warmed Maria. "I will," she promised. And she'd make it up with Connie too. "Cross my heart and hope—"

"Shh," Mamá said quickly, cutting off what shouldn't be said.

When she got to the Khans' place, Maria was still filled with the optimism that came from Mamá's words. When Connie opened the door to Maria and Emilio, Maria said, "Hi, Connie," just as bright and cheery as she could manage it.

Connie muttered, "Hi." Maria explained her errand, feeling her hopes wane.

Connie's mamá spoke kindly enough to her. Carmen Khan, sure enough, sent along all her children, along with Janie, who had come over with her own junk collection.

As the band set out from the Khan house, Connie glowered at Maria. Janie looked down at her sack. They straggled along the river and into town. Up and down the sidewalks and cross streets. Past the Toot-N-Tell 'Em on Bridge Street, toward the north end of town and the collection center. Between them they carried, dragged, and pushed an assortment of sacks, boxes, and barrows filled with clanging pots and pans, tins cans, and even a couple of old tires.

From an open window along the way came music, crackling out from a radio somewhere inside. "Today's the day that all us cats/Must surely do our bit." The song had bounced over the airwaves for a couple of years now, urging everybody to "get some cash for your trash." Fats Waller might have been singing straight at the kids of Yuba City. The ration stamps were as good as cash. It was all about doing "our bit."

Maria and Emilio pushed and pulled the old rusty wagon along. The sacks of tin cans grew heavier with each step. Maria had to stop and tug the wagon across the cracked sidewalk until her arms ached from the effort.

Connie trudged behind Maria with Janie at her side. The four stepladder Khan kids traipsed behind Emilio. The twins raced around. Papi always called them ik-do because one always came with the other, one-two. Connie's little brothers and sisters chattered away, with Emilio joining in, occasionally prompting Connie to warn, "Keep your hands to yourself, Ali," or "Don't pull his hair, Sarah."

Janie talked to nobody, and other than Emilio complaining that she was walking too fast, nobody talked to Maria. The not-talking got into Maria's head and echoed there, threatening to explode like a firebomb if she didn't do something. It got so she didn't care what anyone thought of her. She had to say something.

She turned. She said, "I didn't mean—" at the very same time that Connie said, "Did you hear—?"

Both of them were talking to Janie. Connie was not speaking to Maria, but still, she was speaking, which was better than not.

Janie's eyes widened.

But then . . . But then . . .

She looked away. What did she do that for? Did she not want Maria to talk to her? Was that it? It wasn't Connie, was it? It was her. Maria.

But then Maria noticed something. Janie's eyes were fluttering up the road, across to the Safeway, resting anywhere but upon Maria. Or Connie. Or any of them. Which was when a kind of understanding clickety-snapped in Maria's mind. She wasn't mad. Janie was scared. *Of me?* she thought. *Of what I'll say? How could that be? Or maybe she's afraid of what she'll say back to me?*

Maria's own fears vanished like the mist burned off by sunlight over the Feather River.

"I have to go to the Safeway to turn in my fat jars." She held one up, full of nasty congealed lard. The fat had been used over enough times to turn it murky. That was what you were supposed to do.

"I'll come with you," said Connie.

"I'll come too," Janie whispered.

They crossed the road together in a jangle of metal-filled sacks and the bump-bump-bump of wagon wheels on tarmac.

At the entrance to the Safeway, Maria almost ran right into someone coming out with a shopping bag over one arm. "You can't take all that trash in there," said Doña Elena, her square body blocking the entrance like a tank.

"Oh. Well then, we'll just leave it outside." Maria parked the overloaded wagon against the wall and gathered up the jars of fat.

"You want somebody walking by to take all your stuff?" Doña Elena demanded, and promptly stationed herself beside their cache. "Go on, go on, I'll keep an eye on it for you." Doña Elena always kept an eye on other people's business. Whenever she came to visit Connie's mamá, Connie did her best to eavesdrop. It was a good way to find out everything about everybody.

The Khan kids lined their bags up next to Maria's and Emilio's, and Janie put down the tire she was lugging.

"Never mind, don't thank me," said Doña Elena. "I'm just helping you out for your mamá's sake, from the goodness of my heart."

"Gracias," Maria muttered, knowing that if she didn't, she'd never hear the end of it. They left their trash outside the store in Doña Elena's tender care, and hurried in to find the butcher.

The meat counter was deserted. A poster urged customers to save waste fats for explosives. A pound of fat, it said, would yield enough glycerine to fire four thirty-seven-millimeter antiaircraft shells and bring down one Nazi plane.

Maria knocked on the counter. "We got fat!" she cried.

A harried face appeared—Mr. Slightman, the butcher, a burly man with a face as red as the meats on the table behind him. "How much you got there?" he demanded.

"I don't know—coupla jars."

He wiped his large hands on his bloodied apron, then reached across and took the jars from her. Then he pulled a coin from his pocket and clinked it down upon the counter.

Maria snatched it up. A silver coin. A whole dime? But turning it over, she was disappointed to find the giveaway wheat stalks on the back. Just a wartime penny.

Mr. Slightman gave a belly laugh. "Sorry, little girl," he said. "It's only a steelie. Got to watch out. Had a man in here tried to buy a dime box of corn flakes with one of them yesterday."

But somewhere between the store entrance and the meat counter, something cold and frozen between the girls had thawed out. Pocketing the steel penny, Maria said, "I'm sorry." And she was able to look Janie in the eye as she said it.

Janie did not reject the apology. Neither did she say, Sorry for what? Not everything needed to be said. Some things played out like silent music, between and beneath the words.

Walking past the shelves of flour and tinned goods, Janie said, "My mom wants us to go back to Mexico."

Mexico? Mamá had often talked about taking them there, but not for good. Never that. A visit would be nice, but forever? It was another country. Closer than India, true. But in many ways, as foreign feeling. "You want to go to Mexico?" she asked.

Janie said, "No. But if Mamá goes, then what am I supposed to do? And graduation's coming up and Gloria doesn't even have a dress."

Connie and Maria looked at one another. "What about Bauji?" said Maria. "Who's going to look after him? If you all go away?"

Connie said, "Maybe she'll change her mind." But her voice was the false, high voice of someone who is just trying to make a person feel better.

And now it was Maria who had nothing to say. It was

almost a relief to go back out into the warm day and find Doña Elena—raiding their sacks!

"Hey!" Emilio cried in protest.

Doña Elena brandished a battered saucepan at him, and he stepped back in alarm. "You're not giving those away," Doña Elena said threateningly. "You tell your Mamá I'm taking 'em. Los ladrones!" She picked out another saucepan, a Dutch oven, and three lids. She shook her fist at the thieving government that wanted to snatch everything away from people. "Pots and pans!" she said. "I never heard of such a thing. What next? They'll be wanting our children!"

She made a grabbing gesture at Emilio who shrank back with a gasp. Maria resigned herself to an emptier sack.

"And you, my angel," Doña Elena said, enveloping Janie before she could get away. Janie practically disappeared, emerging breathless and red in the face only when Doña Elena saw fit to release her. "I'm saying a rosary for you and your family. No, no, don't thank me, just take it from the goodness of my . . ."

They left her there in a blaze of piety, and headed up the street to the Associated service station at the intersection of Sumner and Plumas. A billboard proclaimed that if your floorboards were dusty and you wanted a free whiskin', all you had to do was drive right in.

The service station took tires and tin cans from every child who'd hauled them in. "Weapons for our boys," said the mechanic, paying Maria with the precious ration book stamps. Emilio staggered up with his load of cans.

"Whoa, little man," said the mechanic, and he counted out the stamps—blue for processed foods and red for meat, cheese, and butter. "Don't forget to turn in your waste fats. You know what they say, 'Pass the grease and make the ammunition!'"

"Yes, sir," Emilio said. He looked so solemn clutching the stamps in his hand that Maria laughed, and soon they were all laughing, even Janie. Laughing together felt good.

Several young men from the migrant labor camp pulled up in a truck at the collection center and proceeded to unload their trash. They collected their stamps, tipping their caps.

The children, with the men from the camp close behind, headed next to the strip of sidewalk in front of the service station, where Boy Scouts (Troop 17, neat in khaki with their scarves knotted around their necks) collected old beat-up pots and pans. A sign behind them read Sutter County's Aluminum for National Defense.

The scoutmaster chatted with anyone who'd listen about the latest war news. "There's been a Japanese air raid on the Eastern Front," he said. "One of our carriers was damaged."

The Boy Scouts groaned. One of them proclaimed that if the war was still on when he turned sixteen, he'd be signing up like a shot, yessir, he would.

"We got fearsome enemies, no question," another kid said. "The Jerries, the Japs, even them Eye-talians."

"God bless America," the scoutmaster said.

"God bless," the children murmured, all of them and Maria too. Bless America and stop this war. At that moment, Maria hated the Japs (no, Japanese) and the Jerries (no, Germans) and the Italians and all. She hated everyone who had put Janie in this place of half here and half not, one parent dead and the other with her heart broken and her sister with no graduation dress and her grandpa who had once fought in a war and possibly even killed the enemy. Hate drove Maria's thoughts. It buzzed inside her, growing as fast as the flies that appeared from nowhere when something died on the farm.

CHAPTER FOURTEEN

How Many Ways

MAMÁ WAS SO DELIGHTED WITH THE EXTRA RATION stamps that she let Emilio play with them for a whole hour before putting the stamp sheets away in the drawer with the ration book.

Maria attacked Saturday afternoon's endless chores. She was surprised to find that the harder she pummeled the rough soap into the laundry and the higher she flung the sheets over the clotheslines, the farther away the grown-up problems of war and death, countries and freedom, papers and land, receded. She decided she would not think about these things, because what could she do about them? Nothing. Purely nothing. So she pretended that each smack of wet cloth was really a ball smacking into her gloved hand, or the thwack of a bat as she swung. It almost worked. Almost.

Sunday dawned overcast, then turned breezy and bright. By the time everyone was dressed and ready for church, only a few small clouds scudded across the sky, a good sign for the picnic to come.

There was so much to do. Load the food onto the truck. Load the kerosene stove and a tin kettle for heating the coffee. Maria worked alongside Papi and Mamá while Emilio fooled around. He clutched his throat and gargled in joyful imitation of the last dramatic tragedy that had occurred at church on a Sunday, just a few months before.

"Stop that," Maria said.

Emilio protested, "But that's how he—you know!" The old priest at the Iglesia de Santa Rosa had collapsed just so in the middle of Easter Sunday Mass. The imitation was energetic enough that Emilio lost his balance, landed on his bottom in the dust, and got the hiccups.

Papi picked Emilio up and whacked him on the rear end, stopping the hiccups and raising peals of laughter instead. "Enough silliness," Papi said.

Something was missing from the Sunday routine. "Papi, we're not taking your drum?" Maria asked.

"Not today."

No drum. So eating after Mass was allowed, but no dancing. Today, in this church that was meant specially for the adha-adha community, with only a few other people attending from scattered Mexican families in the valley, it was a day to remember a fallen warrior. That's how everyone was talking about Janie's dad. Fallen warrior. Dead hero. It was meant to be praise, but what was the use?

She got into the bed of the truck, lined with a blanket to keep their Sunday clothes clean. She helped Emilio up. Their parents waited, looking up the road. Tía Manuela should have been here by now.

"Can we get me my stamp today?" Emilio asked, fingering the hole in the lining of his cap where he stuck loose change so it collected above the visor and clinked and jingled when he ran. Among his collections were a few postage stamps.

"It's Sunday," Maria said. "The post office won't be open. What stamp do you want now?"

"Nickel stamp," he said. He kept a keen eye out for new postage stamps, which he was allowed to keep, unlike the blue and red varieties that went toward rations. "Papi told me it was on the radio."

"The United Nations stamp?" she teased. "On the radio?"

"They told about it, silly," Emilio said. "It's blue." Blue was his favorite color.

"Isn't Tía coming?" Maria asked.

"We can wait for a few more minutes," Papi said.

Mamá looked anxiously up the road. "I don't see her," she said. "And we never heard from her. I wonder what happened?" She blew a strand of hair off her face as she got in beside Papi and clanged the door shut. Mamá looked tired. Maria had never noticed her looking tired before.

"Better go," said Papi. He started up the truck, making it shudder. They were pulling away when Emilio began to leap up and down in the truck bed. "Stop! Papi, Papi, stop, stop, stop!"

Papi ground the gears in alarm. "Emilio! What happened?"

"It's Tía!" Emilio shouted in delight. "It's Tía Manuela!"

She hurried up the road from the bus stop, clutching a handbag with big brass clips on the side. "Gracias, Kartar!" She scrambled into the back with the children. "Glad I made it."

Papi shook his head at Mamá's crazy sister. Between the hugs and kisses flying around, Maria gathered that Tía had gotten a night pass. She'd tried to send a telegram, but for some reason they were not going through, so she just had to get on the bus and get here, hoping she'd make it in time. She was breathless and happy, and she made Maria breathless and happy as well. "Thank goodness," Tía said, "I caught you before you all went off without me."

They pulled into the uneven gravel lot at church to find children spilling out of all the trucks and cars. The parents hugged and shook hands with one another, while the children skipped around, unleashed. They chased each other around the small plain building, through the flat yard with its thinning grass and picnic tables, and between the gravestones in the cemetery on the west end. Nobody stopped them. Nobody scolded.

The aunties teased a couple of the young Punjabi men from the labor camp who had come along, invited by one or another of the uncles. "You come to Yuba City to find yourself a nice wife?"

"You sure you didn't leave a beautiful bride behind in your homeland, a handsome fellow like you?"

"He was only a baby when he came, Lupe!"

"Too young for you, honey, you stick with the one you got."

The young men laughed bashfully and twisted their caps in their hands as the aunties laid into them.

"How about this one, hah?" They patted Tía Manuela on the arm and chucked her under the chin.

"No, no, señora," Tía laughed them away. "You better go match make for some other girl."

Soon it was confession time. The confessional was in a separate little room, which left the chapel open so the women could make it ready for Mass. They put the flimsy prayer booklets in place and dusted the pews. Candles? Flowers? The padre could not have held Mass without the work of all these women.

Confession today was near torture for Maria, but Father Gonzales didn't seem to notice. For hiding the truth from Mamá and Papi, for disliking Elizabeth, for neglecting Emilio, the priest prayed for her and gave her a Nuestro Padre and three Ave Marias, which was nothing! Vastly relieved, she dashed back into the chapel.

Maria and Emilio sat in a pew toward the front with Mamá and Papi and Tía Manuela. All around, men talked and the padre ushered them into church, and that too was different on this day. Papi and the uncles usually stayed outside. Papi would joke, *Padre, God is everywhere, so I will just pray to him out here, under this beautiful sky!* And the women would roll their eyes at their stubborn heathen husbands. But today the men came inside without a murmur. They sat awkwardly while the women tugged the boys' collars and fixed lace handkerchiefs on the girls' heads. A baby wailed. A toddler's sudden whisper was hushed.

Then Janie and her mamá and her sister, Gloria, made their way slowly up the aisle, and who was leaning on whom, it was hard to tell. The girls' dresses were tidy but mended, and all their clothes wore the faded smoothness that comes from too much wear. Behind them shuffled old Bauji.

Everyone hushed. All but Doña Elena, who was not the hushing sort. "Was he ever baptized?" Her too-loud whisper carried through the building. Neither Janie nor her mother blinked. Gloria wiped her eyes. The priest frowned at Doña Elena. She crossed herself hurriedly.

Tía put her hand over Maria's and held it tight. When Maria looked up she saw her aunt's eyes were misting up.

The padre walked up to the altar, casting a careful eye over this unruly flock. Silence settled. The opening prayers began in this special service in memory of Janie's papa, and whether he was baptized seemed not to matter.

The sun slanting through the windows lit up squares on the walls and shone upon the face of Jesus, patient and sad, and of Mary, his Holy Mother, her hand raised in gentle blessing.

The padre's voice was grand as he talked about the dead man's commitment to his family and community. Maria felt the words floating up and down and all around and they almost brought forgiveness, almost made her think that everything was going to be all right again. You couldn't bring a dead man back but you could remember him. Maybe the priest was right. Maybe grieving together for a good man, in the presence of the Holy Mother Church, did bring you closer to the Lord.

But in the pew ahead, Janie's mother sank into sobs, while her older daughter tried to comfort her. Janie herself sat stiffly, her back ramrod straight, her shoulders unmoving. How many different ways could a person be sad? Emilio's sadness went straight into his angry fists. *Me, I am the opposite,* Maria thought. *When I am angry, I cry, however much I wish I didn't.* Maybe anger and sadness always went hand in hand, slipping one into the other. But now grief had dropped its bombshell upon Janie, and it was unfair, so unfair. Maria found herself blinking back tears. Did life have to throw curves as tough as this one? No amount of blessing, of families, of heroes, of America, was going to give Janie's daddy back to her.

CHAPTER FIFTEEN

Hands with a Story

AFTER COMMUNION, EVERYONE GOT BACK INTO their trucks and drove the short distance to the picnic area at Los Picachos. Usually the Mexican Hindu families talked over each other at the tops of their voices, a small, tight community in the larger world that did not understand them. Today, the conversation was subdued. Even Tía Manuela was quiet, her laughter dampened. The sun shone cheerfully upon those low hills west of the valley that Papi called the smallest mountain range in the world.

The aunties clustered around Janie's mom and talked to her in low voices as the girls drifted away from the grown-ups, from the little kids, and from the teenagers who huddled in their own groups.

Connie and Maria and Janie wandered down the trail

with wildflowers blooming on either side. Connie found a ladybug, and they passed it solemnly from hand to hand.

"Do you hate them?" Maria asked suddenly. "The enemy, I mean." They were speaking again now, friends once more, which was a comfort.

Janie handed the ladybug back to Maria. "I do," she said. The little insect walked down her wrist and dropped into Maria's hand. "You'd hate them too," Janie said. "If it was you."

Silence. The legs of the ladybug tickled. It was a light, sweet touch.

"He wanted to go," Janie said. "He figured if he did, then when he came back, they would let him become an American."

"'They?'" Maria said. "You mean the government."

"That's right," said Janie. "That was what he wanted more than anything."

The ladybug walked across Maria's hand and onto her wrist.

Connie said. "Did you hear about the Germans?"

"The prisoners?" Maria said.

"Yeah. They were trying to get to the Mexican border, but instead they got lost and turned around. Sheriff's deputies tracked them down."

"Where?"

"Up near Chico. They tried to run, and the deputies shot at them. Wounded one, but the other got away."

The ladybug danced its way up Maria's arm and inside her sleeve.

"They shoulda killed him," Janie spat out.

Maria grabbed at the ladybug. She grabbed too hard. When she opened her hand, instead of the whir of open wings, the ladybug lay dark and still.

Maria took a quick, sharp breath. She'd killed it! She hadn't meant to.

"They shoulda killed them both," Janie said.

Maria let the small dead thing fall into a bed of crimson poppies. This is death, she thought, and felt a pang inside her. *I didn't know this before and now I do and it hurts. You can be alive and then life can snap away from you so fast.* Too fast. And how terribly easy it was to make a mistake like this one, to crush a life without intending to. It was only a little beetle, so why did it leave her feeling so empty?

Silence enveloped Los Picachos. "I suppose I would hate them too," Maria said at last. "The enemy. I would so, if it was me."

More silence. Then finally, "Better go back," Connie said. "They'll be calling us to come eat in a minute."

They retraced their steps, down, down this smallest of mountains, along the trail flanked by wild poppies and back toward the picnic tables.

"Do you know what else?" Janie said in a low voice. "Do you know who else is German?"

Maria gaped at her. "Who?"

"Becker," she said, biting out the name. "Arnold Becker."

Becker? Elizabeth's dad? "But they are American," Maria said. "Aren't they?"

They looked at each other. Connie shrugged. "Her dad's people came from Germany," she said. "That's why they had to go to Sharp Park."

"Sharp Park?" said Maria. "That's a military base or something, isn't it?"

"They had to go show their papers to the government, Doña Elena said." Connie added that she thought this was all in case, you know, the Beckers were spies or something.

"A spy?" Maria said. "How can Elizabeth be a spy? She is eleven years old."

Connie insisted that was why the government was keeping an eye on all German and Japanese people and even the Italians. They were enemy aliens, Connie said. Maria thought of the faces she couldn't remember, the kids from those disappeared Japanese families—the Ebiharas, the Yamates. They were just kids. How could they be enemies?

Janie said, "How can they make us play ball with that girl?"

When they got back to the grown-ups, Janie's mom was looking less tearful, Tía Manuela was handing out plates to everyone, and the conversation was rippling along. Doña Elena was talking of her own ill fortune, which was what she usually did. "Be lucky if your man don't have no other wife in some foreign land, and a whole family too that you gotta send money for."

Mamá said Doña Elena's life was full of sad stories. Not only did her present husband insist on supporting that whole other family back in India, but she'd once before been married to a no-good useless gringo who left her with mountains of bills to pay and a son named Albert.

Tía stuck a plate into Maria's hand. While the food smells curled into the air, Maria perched on the edge of a bench and picked at the pollo murghi on her plate, the dish with the funny name that you could only understand if you knew it repeated itself in Spanish and Punjabi, chicken chicken.

Tía came and sat next to her, "What's new, m'ija?"

The plate nearly tipped over. Tía caught it. "Want to talk?" They found a spot behind a big rock, away from the others. Tía settled down cross-legged on the rough grass, drawing her pretty polka-dotted skirt down around her ankles. Maria leaned up against the rock, letting its shade cool her.

They talked—about Becker and the land, about why Papi couldn't buy it. About Emilio getting into fights and Mamá making her walk him home. About Elizabeth and her father and the escaped German prisoners, about Janie's mamá wanting to move the kids to Mexico.

Tía seemed to know most of it already. She said, "It's tough times, Maria. But at least you're playing ball, right?"

Maria nodded. It was true. She was. She scratched at the scab that had formed on her leg from the last fall. Would she ever be free of scabby knees and scratched shins?

"What about those shorts?" Tía asked.

Maria shook her head. "Mamá said she'll show me how to sew a pair. That's great, but I need them tomorrow. I don't know how long Miss Newman's going to let me play in my stupid dress."

"Can't you just get a pair for now?" Tía said. "Borrow them from someone?"

The scab fell off and under it the clean skin was growing. "Sure," Maria said. "I could borrow a pair from Connie."

"Then borrow them!" Tía Manuela threw her hands up in the air. "Come on, honey, you can't keep waiting for the world to serve you ice cream in a silver bowl."

Maria sighed. She had to admit that she was not crazy about wearing shorts made from a pillowcase. And that admission made her cringe, because it made her, really, no better than Elizabeth. She decided that shorts were shorts. Connie's were better than nothing.

Mamá always scolded Maria for not stopping to think. *But here I am, thinking,* said Maria to herself. *I am thinking of all kinds of things, am I not? About how to make something happen when you want it badly. And does that mean, then, that Mamá does not know everything?* The possibility gave her a little shock.

"Thank you," she said. "Gracias, Tía."

"De nada," Tía said. "Did you get my last postcard? Big shiny orange on it?"

"No."

"Look for it," Tía said. "Come on. Let's go back before they figure out we're plotting the revolution."

"Revolution?"

"Girls playing ball," Tía said. "That's a shake-up, isn't it?"

She squeezed Maria's hand with her own callused one. She winked at her and walked back with her, dotted skirt swishing from side to side.

Maria helped Tía open the bottles of RC Cola while Papi and the uncles talked about big things. War. Peace. Freedom. Freedom for India. Ahmed Uncle had brought the sweet, fizzy sodas. He ran a restaurant in town that served adha-adha food, and the manager of the soda factory in El Centro owed him a favor, so these came cheap.

The questions flew as the uncles talked over and around and in between each other. Would it be better when the war ended? Was it not just a white man's war? "That's right. You think India will be free after the war?" "You think we'll be American citizens by then?" "No chance, brother!" "No, no, listen. Dalip Singh Saund says we must have hope." "Did you sign his petition?"

Dalip Singh Saund was a lettuce farmer from Imperial Valley who had been campaigning to get the immigration laws changed. Papi had great respect for him. He was educated, Papi said. He knew how to get things done. Some of the uncles had signed the petition. Others were not so sure.

Someone said, "It will take a revolution to bring change to this country."

A revolution? Was that not what Tía Manuela talked about, plotting revolution?

"I signed," Papi said. "Ahmed signed. Believe it."

Someone else said, "It'll happen. Kartar's right."

The voices wove in and out of each other, growing suddenly silent only when someone said, "Giani. Poor Gian, giving his life for this country." *This country.* Not "his" country or "our" country. How complicated it all was. Had Maria known this all along or was she just learning these knotted realities?

The wives did not join in this talk, although they laughed and joked amongst themselves about the men's heated arguments.

"They think they're going to fix the world," Carmen Khan said.

"I don't know about your husband," said Lucy and Dot Garcia's mother, "but I wish mine would fix the plumbing first."

"At least you got indoor plumbing," said Mamá. "We've been waiting for that for years now."

It was all very well for Tía Manuela to call for revolution, but Tía Manuela had escaped already. Reminded of her aunt's hands, callused from work at the airplane factory, Maria examined her own. They were brown and ordinary, with one nail broken where Emilio had closed a door on it by mistake, one fresh bruise—how did she get that? It looked recent but she had no memory of it—and no calluses.

She longed for hands that had a story to tell.

CHAPTER SIXTEEN

A Word for an Enemy

LATE SUNDAY AFTERNOON, MAMÁ GOT BUSY WITH dinner. Papi took a handful of nails and went to work on the window shutters that came loose every once in a while. The little house rang with the blows of his hammer. Tía Manuela had stopped off in town on the way back from church to visit a girlfriend from her high school days. That left Maria responsible for Emilio. At first he stuck to her the way cheatgrass sticks to a sock. Now that she could play at last, now that Mamá was on her side, she had to keep Emilio entertained.

She brought out her old worn softball. She tossed it from hand to hand—*thwack! thwack! thwoop!*—trying to harden her palms so she'd be ready to play. Puppylike, Emilio was happy enough to fetch for her. But then he got bored, and when the Hamilton boy from up the road, Joey, came by and distracted him, he wanted to go play. "You can play," Maria said, "but no fighting."

She watched them for a while, skirting the wall, tossing her ball, still keeping an eye on them. Covering her bases. This wasn't the time to let Emilio out of her sight and get in trouble for it.

The kids scratched hopscotch grids in the dusty road. They seemed to be fine. She threw the ball up higher and higher, catching it—*smack!*—as it came down. She could wander a bit and not be missed, surely. She'd still be able to hear them. Soon she found herself walking along the edge of the irrigation ditch beneath wispy clouds. It was airless and still, the sound of the water in the wide ditch below so hypnotic that it was some time before she took a deep breath of field-scented air and realized she was all the way out in the lettuce plantings. She couldn't see Emilio from here. She'd better turn around and go back.

When she did, she found Emilio and Joey slamming into each other with arms and legs and fists.

"Stop it, you two!" She waded into the thick of the punches as they rolled around in the dirt. She yelled at them both and sent Joey packing.

Emilio went wailing inside to the kitchen, where Papi was hammering a loose floorboard. "Maria won't let me play!"

"Liar!" Wouldn't let him play? "You were trying to kill each other! Papi, him and Joey were kicking and punching each other out there." Would Papi believe her?

Papi did. He scolded Emilio. "Didn't I tell you don't make trouble? What are you doing getting into fights?"

Maria felt Mamá's sharp eyes on her over the bowl of hamburger meat. Would Mamá say it was her fault for not watching Emilio?

"Who started it?" Papi demanded. The very question Mamá had asked Maria.

"Probably that stupid Joey," Maria said, on Emilio's side now, even though she'd shaken him within an inch of his life to stop his flying fists.

Mamá sighed. Then she said, "You be nice to Joey."

"Why?" Emilio demanded. "He wasn't nice to me."

Papi reached out to stroke Emilio's head, then pulled his hand back as if he could not bear to touch his son's cut hair. "That boy's father is away at the front," Papi said.

"Joey's father?" Maria hadn't known.

Papi said, "I don't care what started it off between you boys. But I know Will Hamilton, and he's a good man." He put the hammer away in its toolbox under the stairs. "I have to go now." He kissed Mamá.

Mamá laid her hand on Papi's arm and said, "You're not going to eat first?"

"I'll be back soon," he said, and his eyes rested in warning upon his children, both of them standing there with shreds of promises and intentions falling about them like dry leaves scattered by the wind. "You two stay home and help your Mamá," Papi said. "This fighting has got to stop."

Why me? Maria thought. *Why would Papi look at me this way? I'm not the one who got into a fight.*

The door closed behind Papi. "Where's Papi going?" Maria asked.

Mamá crossed herself. "To talk to Becker."

"The oso? About the orchard?"

"What else?" Mamá didn't even smile at the silly nickname. "And after that, he has a meeting in town."

Becker and then a meeting? If all that put Papi in a temper, what were the odds he'd listen to her? Maria's competing thoughts all scrambled for room and chattered at once. She circled the kitchen, restless from thinking too much.

"Go feed and water the chickens," Mamá said. "You're driving me crazy, walking round and round like that."

"I wanna go water the chickens too," Emilio said promptly.

But Mamá said, "'Milio, take this!" She held a little portion of the hamburger meat to him, all mixed up with breadcrumbs and spices, and he was immediately distracted. He set to work at once, rolling and patting it between his palms.

Mamá nodded at Maria, *Go. Now.* Sometimes Mamá could make herself entirely clear with a quick movement of head and hands, no words needed in any language. Maria grabbed up the bucket full of carrot tops and bean strings, and escaped to the outdoors with only her thoughts for company.

Upon seeing her, the chickens were all in a flutter. As soon as she got in the coop, something feathered flapped onto Maria's head and beat its wings around her ears. She dropped the platter of vegetable scraps, nearly slipping on a piece of lettuce.

"Goofy bird!" Maria pinned the red hen down and battled her back to the ground. She scattered the scraps, emptied the water bowls, and refilled them with fresh water from the pump. The hen hopped up and cocked her head at Maria, blinking her white-rimmed eyes as if trying to decide if she should fly at her again.

"Papi's right," Maria said. "One of these days, it's the curry pot for you."

"You talking to the chickens?"

Maria jumped. "What do you want?" How long had Elizabeth been standing there by the fence, watching her?

"Came to give you this." Elizabeth held out a battered copy of a magazine. "Mailman brought it to us by mistake yesterday." Maria shook off carrot peel and bean scraps, and extracted herself from the coop. Elizabeth held the magazine in a two-finger grip at the end of her outstretched arm, the way a person holds something that smells bad.

It was a copy of *La Familia* that Mamá ordered for patterns. "Thank you." Maria tried to keep her voice even.

"It's not English," Elizabeth said.

"It's Spanish," Maria replied. A small, wicked impulse nudged her to add, "You can't read it."

Silence. Then, "Why in the world would I want to read it?" Elizabeth said.

Maria snapped. "Yeah, you wouldn't, would you, German girl?" She hadn't meant to say it quite like that, but that was how it came out, and it was too late to undo the words.

Elizabeth gave a great, choking gasp. Her face flushed red. She turned and ran in stumbling, awkward steps, kicking up the dust behind her.

Maria went inside the house. She should have felt righteous, but instead she felt like a criminal. She gave the magazine to Mamá.

"Mail on a Sunday?" Mamá said. "Where did you get this from?"

Maria explained. She said nothing about Elizabeth's gibe, nor her own swift retort. Nothing about Elizabeth's reaction, nor the strange lack of satisfaction that came from giving as good as she'd gotten.

"That poor girl," Mamá said.

"Elizabeth? Why?"

Mamá flipped through the magazine, muttering under her breath about men who paid no attention to what was under their noses. She said, "He's been different since his wife died, that man."

"Who?"

"Who do you think? Señor Becker, that's who."

"Why?"

"Maybe his daughter is a reminder," said Mamá. "Of his dead wife. You'd think that would make him kinder to her, but the mind is a wicked thing sometimes."

Maria gaped at her, stricken. The mind. A wicked thing, surely.

"It's a hard enough life," Mamá said, "without people being mean to each other."

"Yes," said Maria, uncertain where this was going.

"Meanness breeds meanness," Mamá said. "You remember that."

For a moment, Maria's heart flipped right over from guilt. But Mamá, mind reader though she might be, merely flapped a page open. "What do you think?" She tapped a dress pattern. It looked pretty and frilly.

"Who's it for?" Maria asked suspiciously.

"Graduation dress. Doña Elena didn't give me patterns for all of them."

Not just hems anymore. Mamá was sewing whole dresses for bad-tempered Doña Elena.

"One more issue left," Mamá said. "After that, no more *La Familia*."

"Why not?"

"Can't afford it," Mamá said.

"We can't?" But Mamá looked forward to each issue of the magazine.

"We have to cut corners. Maybe, someday . . ." They were always saving. For the future. For the children. Mamá said, "She'll have to give me patterns if she wants me to sew."

Maybe, someday? What did Mama mean? Maybe, someday we can get *La Familia* again? But no, Maria suspected that Mamá was banking on another faraway someday. When a miracle would happen and the laws would change. If Papi was ever in a hundred years allowed to buy the land he worked, Mamá was going to be dead sure he had the money for it.

Maria leafed through the sewing patterns in the magazine. The wide skirts and pretty flounces of the graduation dresses distracted her briefly, reminding her of Janie's sister, Gloria. Not for long, though. She was looking for something else.

"Since when did you get interested in sewing?" Mamá said.

"I don't know."

Mamá gave her a sharp look. "I think I know," she said. Maria met Mamá's eye, and it was as if Mamá could read her inside out. But then Mamá's face softened. She said, "Give me some time, and we'll see about your pants."

"Shorts," said Maria. "I'll sew them. If you'll show me how."

"I'll show you," said Mamá.

"What about Papi?" said Maria.

"We'll see," said Mamá.

Papi returned from his talk with Becker and his other mysterious meeting and would say nothing to anyone about either. Tía Manuela came back from her visit with her girlfriend in town, and she too seemed quiet.

At dinner, when they were all seated around the big wooden kitchen table, Emilio said, "Papi, will you tell us a story?"

But Papi said, "No more stories about Punjab. You are Americans, and it's time to put all that behind us."

For one long, hollow moment, Emilio stared at his father. Then he burst into tears. Tía Manuela rushed to his side. She put her arms around him. Emilio sobbed, "Papi— story," and would not be comforted.

Papi stuck his lower lip out and glared at both Emilio and Tía. For one glimmer of a moment, Maria could see how much Papi and Emilio were alike. Where else did

Emilio get that stare from, that very same set of his chin when he wanted to get his own way?

Mamá shook her head as if she couldn't figure Papi out. But Tía Manuela said, "Kartar, what's wrong with stories? You want Hortensia to quit telling them too?"

Papi glowered. "I'm the one who always told them," he said. "But no more. No more of that nonsense. No old stories, as if we can go back to that old life every time some little thing goes wrong. We are here. This is our life. That's it."

Maria wanted to cry, *What's wrong with stories?* She wanted to say, *Look at Emilio's face. Look at me! Look at us, Papi!* She longed to have the old Papi back, and she had no way of saying this. That empty place opened up in her. More taking away. How much more taking away could they all stand?

Tía Manuela said, "I can tell you stories about Mexico, 'Milio. And Los Angeles."

But Emilio's mouth still drooped. *Tell me a story, Papi.* Papi had always told stories when they asked him to. Always, but no more now?

Later, over suds and dishwater, Mamá said, "Nobody is so stubborn as Kartar."

"He's punishing the children," Tía Manuela said, "because the world is punishing him. That is not fair."

Maria scrubbed the bottom of the frying pan until her hands ached.

"Once he gets something into his head," Mamá said, "none of us can stop him."

It was true. *If Papi ever fell in the river,* Maria thought gloomily, *count on it, you'd have to look for him upstream.* But behind the gloom she recognized something else. Mamá was not defending Papi. Mamá was not taking his side. Not in this. Not this time.

As she usually did when she visited, Tía Manuela slept in Maria's room at the top of the stairs. They settled in on the unfolded mattress, and Tía combed Maria's hair, brushing comfort into her with every stroke. "Shall I tell you a story?" she said softly.

Maria nodded.

"There were once two girls with dreams who came with their parents to California from Mexico. The older one was a clever girl. She wanted to graduate high school. She wanted to work and make her own money. But she had to help her papi in the fields, picking the lettuce and beans. She had to help her mamá in the kitchen, canning the peaches. They could not spare her. There was not enough time for school, so she dropped out."

"Mmm?" Maria murmured drowsily. She knew this story.

"When she grew up, still working in those fields, she met a kind man from a faraway place. He fell in love with her. He courted her with bags of peaches and bunches of wildflowers. She was charmed by his flashing eyes and by how kind he was to her. They married. They had two beautiful children."

Maria lifted her head.

"Only her family didn't like the fact that he was foreign— not Mexican, not even American."

"This is us," Maria said. "Papi and Mamá."

"From her whole family, only one sister would speak to this young, dreaming woman."

"You?"

"Me. Because your Mamá dropped out, I got to go to school. I got to graduate. Your Mamá made my dreams come true, Maria." Tía's eyes blazed with fire. "And guess what? Your Mamá's still dreaming. Only her dreams are now for you. That you will be a good, strong person. That you will be happy."

Maria blinked. "All I want to do is play ball."

Tía put the brush down. "Wanting something," she said, "is not enough. You have to work for it."

As she fell asleep that night, Tía Manuela's words in her ears, Maria thought she heard her parents talking behind the wall of their bedroom.

"Kartar, you have to . . . This is America!"

Papi's voice, saying something urgent and insistent.

Mamá: "This is not Mexico and it is not your India. When will you learn?"

The words mixed together in her mind with others from the day just past, all clouded up so Maria could hardly tell if she was remembering them or dreaming them. Tía's words: good . . . and happy . . . *you can't keep waiting for the world to serve you ice cream in a silver bowl.*

Elizabeth's voice crept in as well, from earlier in the day. *It's not English . . . . Why in the world would I want to read it?* So much dislike. So much contempt. And Maria's own words, in vicious reply. *German girl.* Words for an enemy. Maria's mind shifted restlessly from good and happy to fearful and hopeless, from taking charge and making do to being mad and getting even. Finally, she sank into sleep.

CHAPTER SEVENTEEN

How Long?

WHEN MARIA AWOKE ON MONDAY MORNING, GETTING even didn't seem so important. Tía had left already, but her words lingered behind her along with the Lux soap smell on Maria's pillow. Good and happy. Was it possible to be both? Maybe so, now that she didn't have to lie. She could go to ball practice without hiding it anymore from Mamá and Papi. She would become a new Maria, fearless and brave in this newly dawning week.

Drawing water with Mamá at the pump, Maria said, "What about my shorts? Did Papi say anything?"

Mamá yanked the handle of the water pump, pursing her lips. "Oh yes."

"And? What?"

Mamá shook her head. "Never mind," she said. "We'll make you those shorts if you need them."

"We will?" *So never mind Papi?* She didn't say that, but that's what it sounded like. It flew in the face of everything she knew to be true about her parents. They disagreed about plenty, but in the face of questions from their children they were always united.

"We will." Mamá pressed her lips together. "In time."

"But Mamá—"

"That's enough, Maria," Mamá said.

What about today? And tomorrow? Hefting the bucket of water for Mamá, walking back to the house without slopping, Maria decided she had better handle today and tomorrow in her own way.

No more lies. That thought remained on Maria's mind through the school day. During reading, she whispered to Connie, "Is it still okay if I borrow your shorts?"

"Tomorrow." Connie grinned at her. "I'll bring the extra pair to school."

No more meanness. Maria kept a sideways eye on Elizabeth, who did not give her even a single look. She wanted to say, *I'm sorry,* but there did not seem to be a good time for that.

●●●

Maria managed to play in her dress without falling. She stretched and caught. It was batting practice today. They rotated, with Lucy and Connie pitching, and four girls at a time in the infield. Miss Newman wanted to see them playing different positions while batting practice went on. Maria felt a thrill when she took her place at bat.

A few swings and misses. One pop-up that went right into the dirt. Then *smack!* She connected. She lined the ball between Dot at third and Elizabeth at shortstop, and neither of them could make a play on the ball.

Miss Newman drove them hard. "I don't care if the gloves are in tatters," she cried. "I don't care if you've got sun in your eyes. I'm telling you—you want to play, you learn to keep your eye on that ball!"

It wasn't until afterward they all learned why Miss Newman had turned into such a whirling fury. She called them all together.

"I've got something to tell you," she said, leaning up against the dilapidated brick of the school building, tossing the ball up in the air and catching it with her other hand. "About our ball field. It is possible there isn't going to be one."

They gaped at her, then an outcry erupted, everyone talking and exclaiming at once.

"Listen," she said, hushing them all instantly. "The federal government and the levee district have donated land to the county near the fairgrounds. It appears now the *gentlemen*"—Maria thought only Miss Newman could make that word sound like an insult—"the gentlemen on the board of supervisors have decided that they are going to be using that land for other purposes." Miss Newman stopped and glared at them all, defying anyone to interrupt her. "So our field has been deferred."

The questions erupted. "Defurred?" "What's that mean?" "They're not going to build it?" "Where are we gonna play?"

"It's been postponed!" said Miss Newman, throwing the ball up so high that it seemed to touch the clear blue sky before arcing back down again. She caught it with a resounding smack in her bare hand, and if it hurt—it must have hurt—she made no sign. "It makes no sense. Why not a ball field? There isn't one for miles. But they have made up their minds."

Everybody got to buzzing and talking, which faded into murmurs soon, as if it was obviously no good.

Maria was surprised to hear herself saying, in a slightly croaky voice, "We should tell 'em."

Everyone turned to look at her.

"We should," she said again, and this time she was louder and clearer, no frog in her throat.

"Tell who?" said Lucy at the same time Dot said, "You think they'll listen?"

"You mean the county board," Janie said.

She got it. Janie, with her face that was so drawn and closed these days. Janie with her shirt that needed mending, who looked as if no one paid attention anymore to how she dressed or whether she combed her hair.

Janie said, "Maria's right."

"We should go there when they meet to talk about it," Maria said, her spirits soaring like a cleanly batted fly ball.

And Miss Newman agreed. Miss Newman said that Maria was absolutely right. If they felt strongly about something like this, they ought to listen carefully and talk to their parents. They ought to get their parents to come watch them practice, see why playing ball mattered. They ought to learn how to speak up, raise a point, and be heard, because that was how things worked in a democracy, which was precisely why the United States of America was different from monarchies like Japan and dictatorships like fascist Italy and Nazi Germany. "Think about it," she said. "You just think about it."

Families had come to watch practice that afternoon—some of the girls' older brothers, and Milly Anderson's grandpa, known to all as Gramps. All the Khan kids were there as well. Emilio spent practice time playing with the younger ones. On the way back home, he chattered happily about Connie's brothers and sisters: who could jump the longest, who could toss a coin the highest. All the way home, Maria wondered about this speaking-up that Miss Newman said would be a good and democratic thing to do. The part about parents coming to see the girls play—that point in particular jabbed sharp and steely at her, because what would Papi say when he saw her playing in anything but her modest long skirt? She tried to tell herself she didn't care, but that right there was a lie, she knew. What Papi thought mattered to her. It mattered a lot.

When Maria got home, she found Tía Manuela's postcard had arrived. It had a big shiny orange on it, circled with a wreath of delicate white buds and blossoms and spicy-bright leaves. "Sunny Southern California," said the pale peach-colored lettering that looped around the fruit.

Manuela had written on the back:

> *This one's for Maria.*
> *Be brave. Don't give up.*
> *Love,*
>
> *Tía Manuela.*

Mamá's sewing fingers flew—what a lot Mamá sewed these days. It seemed as if she always had a cloud of cloth in her lap, or was guiding it through the tabletop hand-cranked sewing machine. Papi once said, "Why do they call that machine a Singer when it is just a noisemaker?" But today, Mamá finished a neckline by hand while Papi listened to the news on the radio. He listened to news of the war but really, he listened for the names that made up the news from India—names like Nehru and Gandhi and Patel and others that went by too fast for Maria to understand.

Jab! Jab! Jab! went Mamá's silver needle, in and out of the cloth. Papi listened and listened as if nothing else mattered in the world but the old RCA radio, which was the very first thing he had bought with his very first earnings in Yuba City, after he'd come here from

El Centro when Maria was only a baby. Maria longed to change the station to KMYC in the hope of catching some little fragment about the All-American Girls, but she didn't dare.

Suddenly Papi froze. He twiddled and turned the knob so the volume crackled up higher.

The needle stilled in Mamá's fingers. They all stared at the radio as if something live was going to pop out of it any minute. "British ambassador to the United States, Lord Halifax," said the newsreader's voice, "in a statement to the press today . . ."

"What?" said Maria. "What are you listening to, Papi?"

"Shh!" Papi warned. "Be quiet!"

Maria shrank back. Papi never talked to her like that, as if he meant to cut her voice in half with his own. Emilio looked up with watchful eyes from his place on the floor, where he was playing with Papi's coins from India.

The news item was about a congressman in Washington, Emmanuel something or other, and a bill. India's contribution to the war figured in the news item too, as it rushed by. So Papi was listening to talk about India once more.

After the radio went on to other matters, Papi tried to explain. Last night after his talk with Becker, Papi had gone to a meeting at the El Ranchero Restaurant. Dalip Singh Saund, the Imperial Valley lettuce farmer, had been there. He'd told Papi and the uncles about a congressman in Washington who was on their side. His name was Emmanuel Celler. Papi and the uncles had all signed letters that Dalip Singh was going to send to Washington. "This bill has been defeated before," Papi said, "but Mr. Celler is introducing it again in the House of Representatives."

Mamá crossed herself, and the fingers she touched to her lips hovered there a few extra seconds.

"The bill will allow people from India to become citizens," Papi said.

"Then it'll all be okay," Maria said. "You can buy the house and the land. We can stay here in this house."

"That's good, isn't it Papi?" said loyal Emilio.

Papi did not shush them now. "If it passes," he said. "But how soon? We don't know. These things take time. Dalip Singh said they'll take it to the Immigration Committee. He thinks there is support in the House."

"It can sit there in that committee!" said Mamá. "For months."

"And that is just the House," Papi said. "Then it has to go to the Senate, and God alone knows what will happen there. Already there's a senator from Alabama who has sworn he'll kill it."

"How long . . . ?" Maria began.

Mamá cut in. "Papi doesn't know how long, Maria. It's how the government works." Which meant she could see that Papi was tired and she didn't want Maria bothering him with her questions.

"If Becker wants us to leave now," Papi said, slow and halting as if his thoughts would not easily shape themselves, "then what is the use of all this gup-shup about friendship with India and support for freedom? What's the use of talk?"

Mamá said, "Kartar . . . ." her shoulders hunching with worry.

Papi said, "He's in a hurry, Hortensia. He wants to sell now and go to Sacramento. I can't blame him."

"Can't blame him?" Maria cried, outraged. "How can you say that? He's going to throw us out of this house! What are we going to do? Where will we go?"

Mamá gave Maria a stop it now look. Papi said, "Maria, you would not understand. It's complicated."

Maria cried, "Tell me and I'll try to understand, Papi!"

Mamá and Papi said, together, "Not now, Maria." It was not unkind, but it cut her down to size. It was as if they thought she was too young to understand, which she was not, most definitely.

Emilio stacked coins into a careful pile, glancing at Papi and Mamá out of the corner of his eye.

"Some people want to see enemies everywhere," said Papi, which also made no sense at all. "It's hard to do business in these times."

Mamá thrust the needle into the fabric. She stabbed herself right through it, but did she cry out loud? Not Mamá. She extracted her hand and raised her finger to her mouth, sucking away the welling drop of blood.

Emilio toppled his stack of coins.

"Maybe something will come up," said Papi. But he did not look as if he believed it.

Emilio gathered the coins, brought them to Papi, and offered them with both hands. Papi took them automatically, but his face was creased with that deep, deep frown.

"I'll make some kara-parshad tonight," Mamá murmured. Mostly Papi made the traditional sweet Sikh offering on special holy days, but occasionally Mamá would make it when extra blessings were needed. Then Papi would pray from his holy book and Mamá too would say an Ave Maria. Sometimes life demanded help from every kind of god.

And here Maria had fancied that getting a pair of shorts and playing ball would make her world a perfect place. How could she be brave and not give up when everything was falling to pieces around her?

CHAPTER EIGHTEEN

Unfair

MARIA AND CONNIE BOTH SHOWED UP EARLY TO school the following morning, before the doors had even opened. It just happened that way; they hadn't planned it. Each of them had sticky-burr brothers and sisters in tow. Emilio promptly abandoned Maria to play with the Khan kids. They chased each other, screaming randomly.

"Here you go." Connie brought a small folded bundle out of her book bag. "Shorts for you. Put them in your bag. You can wear them for practice." Maria stuffed the pale cream shorts into her book bag. "Perfect." And they were, pillowcase cloth and all. She dug her ball and glove out. "Want to play some?" She ran to the twisted old avocado tree in the middle of the schoolyard. She turned and threw the first one. It sang through the air.

Back and forth. Back and forth flew Maria's old ball. Connie snatched it up tidily with that nice wide glove of hers. Back and forth, throwing and catching. Kids arriving at school stopped to watch.

Thwump! Thwump! went the ball. Not a miss. Not one, not until the bell rang and Connie's attention wavered, and *Thunk!* went Maria's old ball into the dirt. Connie tucked the glove into her bag. They ran to the school door, laughing together.

But when they got to the classroom, the morning's perfection evaporated like the promise of rain in the dry season. Maria heard Janie saying something to Miss Newman. Her words froze Maria in the doorway with the classroom door still half open.

"They found his body," Janie said.

Whose body? But deep inside, Maria knew.

Miss Newman looked up for a split second before saying, "Give us a minute or two, please, girls." Maria and Connie retreated. They waited in the hallway with that news still ringing in their ears. *They found his body.*

"Gian Uncle," Connie whispered.

Maria had no words.

The rest of the fifth grade had arrived and begun to

chatter among themselves. When Miss Newman opened the door, her face was so solemn and stern that the conversation died down at once.

The morning passed in somber silence. Miss Newman plowed through the subjects of the day with grim determination. No one dared to cross her.

At recess, Connie and Maria followed Janie to the foot of the avocado tree. She went up to the tree and put her face against the bark.

"Janie," they said together.

Janie turned. She looked from one to the other of them. She said, "You heard. It's true."

Around them buzzed voices. The boys played their usual war games—today it was all hospital trains and stretchers, wounded warriors groaning and wheels going clackety-clack. Only some men never made it home.

"Where did they—you know, find him?" Maria asked.

"France." Janie dashed a tear away. "He probably . . . actually . . . passed away—" She stopped and her chin quivered.

"It's okay, Janie," Connie said.

"Months ago," Janie whispered. "Maybe even last year. I don't get it. I don't know how."

"You don't have to talk if you don't feel like it," Maria said. Last year? That was why the letters had stopped coming.

The story came out in small, broken pieces. "He's buried out there—they told us he was MIA—back in January— Mamá didn't believe them."

MIA—missing in action. Connie took both of Janie's hands in her own. Maria put her hands on top of both their hands. They stood like that for a moment under the avocado tree with the unbearable held between them.

"They identified him," Janie whispered, "from the coin in his pocket. Can you believe that?"

"A coin?" said Maria. Surely many soldiers carried coins in their pockets.

Janie nodded. "An Indian coin," she said. Her lips got all twisty. "He was the only one on that whole Normandy beach with one of them."

Maria could almost see it. A coin like Papi's, with the head of the King of England on it. An anna coin or one pice. It was a funny thing, how Papi hated the English king but he loved those Indian coins like old friends. All the uncles did.

As the bell rang for the end of recess, Maria wondered if dying hurt. The bullets hurt, for sure, but what about the moment of dying? She'd seen animals die. She'd even helped Mamá pluck chickens. And that ladybug, how still it went when she crushed it, not meaning to. Maria tried to imagine it all, war and bodies and bullets that killed people. But it was too big, too far, too foreign to make sense.

Normandy. Miss Newman had shown it to them on a map. Maria could still remember the curve of the beaches with the English Channel to the north. Such a faraway place to die. Then again, distances were nothing to Papi and the uncles. They'd all been born in a place so far away it was almost a dreamland.

Heading back in through the school door, Maria decided to focus instead on what was real and here and now. "Janie," she said. "We threw some balls this morning, Connie and me. Wish you'd been there."

Janie looked up.

Connie said, "We'll do it again. Now that we all have gloves and everything."

Janie nodded. "We should oil those gloves," she said. "I can show you how. Jim showed me once." Jim was Janie's sister Gloria's boyfriend, who played baseball at the high school. Talking of these normal things, Janie's lips untwisted.

Oh, life was unfair. It was downright unfair. But even

with all that life was slinging at them, there was softball. Just throwing that ball around with Connie that morning had felt so good. They could still be friends together, Janie and Connie and Maria. They could practice their windups and work at striking each other out. Maybe playing ball could keep your heart from breaking.

CHAPTER NINETEEN

Not the Usual

BY THE BOTTOM OF THE THIRD IN THAT AFTER noon's practice game—just three innings—the boys were winning, 2 to 1. Connie was on second with two outs.

The shorts fit so perfectly that Maria did not even mind the faded fabric. She wondered why she'd ever thought she would.

The boys were strong hitters and they could run. The sun in Lucy's eye made her miss a couple of easy catches. Sometimes the ball would bounce up against a tussock of grass and ricochet in unexpected directions. If you got in the way, you could end up with a nasty blow. There was nothing soft about a softball when it hit you.

Two outs, and then two pitches from Tim. Maria swung. Missed. And again. Missed. Her announcer voice picked up the commentary. *The crowd groans. Maria grips the bat.*

A couple of the little Khans watching yelled, "Come on, Maria!" Lucy and Dot's daddy had come to watch as well. He came now and then like some of the other uncles. The game baffled them, even though they insisted it wasn't that different from cricket, which they'd all played as boys back in India.

The boys were sniggering less now than they had been at first. They'd figured out the girls were serious.

A practice swing or two and then, the pitcher throws. Maria steps up and into her swing, pulls the bat hard around, and now it's going, going . . .

Maria tore off, running as fast as she could.

The ball goes high—it's a pop fly!

Maria's running, running hard. She's digging up the dirt. She heads for first base . . . The left fielder makes a play for the ball and misses narrowly.

Safe at first base! Maria's heart pounded in happiness. A hit! She'd gotten a hit.

Dot was up next to bat. On the very first pitch, she hit a foul ball just behind the plate. The catcher snagged it for the third out. The girls groaned.

Now the boys were in to bat. Lucy pitched. Mondo hit. A long fly. He started running. The ball soared.

Maria spotted that ball. She started to run from her position on second.

Janie ran too. "Mine!" Janie cried from right field, racing up with glove outstretched.

Another voice cried, "I got it!" It was Elizabeth. She'd raced back into the outfield too, from first base, looking up in the sky, watching that ball arc back down.

Maybe they didn't hear each other. Maria stopped short. The bodies thudded.

Miss Newman's whistle blew, wheep-wheep! "Collision!" she called out.

But it didn't stop there. "I called it!" Janie screamed. "I called the ball."

"Didn't you hear me?" Elizabeth shouted back. "I called it too."

From his perch on the fence, one of the little Khans stifled a shriek.

"I called it first."

"You did not."

"Did! I did." Janie wasn't backing down.

Neither was Elizabeth. "Did not—you're lying. Liar!"

She jabbed her finger in the air toward Janie with each word she spoke. "You dirty half-and-half."

Silence. Such a terrible silence. It wasn't the words that hurt. Not exactly. Half-and-half. After all, the Punjabi-Mexican families jokingly called themselves that all the time. But somehow, from Elizabeth, those words exploded like bullets.

"What did you call me?" Janie shrieked.

And then she was throwing herself upon Elizabeth, grabbing her hair with both fists, pushing her down, her face streaked with tears and dirt. "How dare you? How dare you?" Scratching and pulling and tugging, and both of them shrieking. The grunting and yelling made Maria's skin creep. She plunged into the fray, yelling, "Stop it you two! Stop stop stop!"

Over the blast of Miss Newman's whistle, Maria found herself yelling. Connie was yelling too. The world was all dust and noise and the heat and thud of bodies. It was hard to keep from being hit. Maria found herself pushing back, pushing and shoving with arms and legs and body, so that suddenly there was no way to stop.

They were rolling in the dirt now, all four of them, and suddenly there were people all over the field, parents and onlookers and even the principal, Mr. Walker himself. Then Miss Newman was in there, pulling them apart, yelling, "Stop it. Stop it this minute!"

They staggered upright. All those eyes on Maria. She blinked and wiped her sweaty face. Mr. Walker demanded, "What in the world is the explanation for this?"

Maria couldn't think of what to say, couldn't explain why Janie had thrown herself at Elizabeth as if she intended to knock her senseless. She couldn't think. Her body had taken over and her mind could not work. She only knew that when Elizabeth had shouted that horrible name at Janie, she too had felt something mean and hateful stirring inside her. She'd jumped in to stop them fighting, but as for whose side she was on, she did not know.

Elizabeth whined, "Janie started it. She jumped me."

Janie lifted a shoulder to shrug her sleeve back into place. She would not look at anyone. She said nothing.

"You called her a bad name," Connie cried.

"Hush up, now, Connie," said Miss Newman.

They stared at her. What? Connie should hush up? Not a word to Elizabeth? Had Miss Newman not heard what Elizabeth had said?

Miss Newman's eyes met Maria's, and Maria had to look away. "Janie, Maria," said Miss Newman, "do you have something to say?"

Janie said nothing. Maria stared down at her shoes and muttered, "No, ma'am."

"Yes, you do," said Miss Newman. "There is something called an apology."

"Me?" said Maria, outraged. "I should apologize? I was only trying to stop them."

Miss Newman sighed. She reminded them all that playing on a team meant acquiring a team spirit, and there were a few rules. Just a few. "No fighting. No swearing. Treat teammates with respect. Yes?"

Maria said, "Elizabeth didn't treat us with respect."

"If you all want to play sports," said Mr. Walker, putting his two cents in, "then you'll mind your manners on and off the field and behave like ladies."

Miss Newman said softly, "Thank you, Mr. Walker. I can handle this." He nodded and backed off, but he lingered anyway, keeping a wary eye on all of them—the girls for sure, but Miss Newman as well.

"Look, girls," said Miss Newman. "I don't know what's going on between you four." She looked from Janie to

Elizabeth to Maria to Connie. "But any more of this, and you'll all face the consequences. Do you understand me?"

No one said a word. Not even Elizabeth.

Miss Newman said, "In the future, *if* you want to play ball with us—" She paused to make sure they understood that "if."

They nodded, all of them, even Janie and Elizabeth.

"Any time you have a complaint about a teammate, you come talk to me—immediately—and we will sort it out. Nothing like this is allowed to happen during practice again."

Mr. Walker nodded too, satisfied.

The worst of it was, Maria knew that it could have been her pummeling Elizabeth. It felt as if the war had come home.

CHAPTER TWENTY

Wickedly Unfair

PAPI AND MAMÁ SAT WAITING AT THE KITCHEN TABLE. Emilio took one look at their faces and tore straight upstairs. Papi wore a cloud on his face. Mamá was a lightning bolt. "Sit down," Mamá said.

Maria sat.

"I met your teacher at Anderson's Market," Papi said. "She told me you got in a fight."

Mamá said a whole lot more. She talked just the way she beat up rugs at the end of a dusty summer, beat them and beat them and just when you thought she was done, she beat them some more. She said they'd trusted Maria, trusted her and this was how she repaid that trust? It was impossible to believe, she said. What a blow to her and to Papi to find this out! "Papi just met your teacher by chance.

You got in a fight? A fight? ¡Dios mío! My daughter getting in a fight? Jesús y Maria, I never thought I would live to see that day!" And on and on.

Maria tried to speak up but it was useless. When Mamá got that way, all you could do was stand aside and hope the flood would ebb out by itself. When it finally did, Mamá sat up straight, clasped her hands together, and said, "I don't know what to do now."

"Can I say something?" Maria said.

"Yes," said Papi. "But it better not be an excuse."

"Papi," Maria said. "It's not. At least, I don't think it is." She explained the fight, how something very common had happened, something that could easily happen anytime in a game. Two players running into each other, each of them thinking that she alone had called the ball. Only when these two players collided, it led to disaster.

Papi and Mamá looked at each other. Then Papi said, "Your teacher said there was name calling. She said two other girls started it but you joined in. Is that true?"

Maria took a deep breath. "Well, yes, Papi, but there's more." She told them about how she had jumped in to separate them. She told them everything. Even the words. The terrible words that had started it all.

Her parents exchanged looks once more. Mamá took a long, sharp breath in between her teeth. "That Elizabeth," she said. "That girl is nothing but trouble."

"Still," Papi said. "You were there, Maria, and you were on the ground fighting, no? This is what your teacher saw."

Maria had to admit, yes, that was true.

"Did you hit anyone?"

"I don't know," Maria said, truthfully. "It was very confusing."

"Fighting," Papi said, "is always confusing. But tell me this. In your heart? How did you feel?"

Maria admitted that she did not feel good. That she had rushed in to stop them fighting but that in the process, she herself had pushed and shoved and she may even have landed a blow or two.

"That's what I thought," Papi said. "How will you pay for this, Maria?"

"I don't know," Maria said, but she was ready to make amends. "I'll do the laundry. I'll scrub the kitchen floor." She'd pulled a muscle in her shoulder for sure. It nagged her, uneasy as a conscience. The fight would be worth a rosary or two at confession.

"Maria can help me with my sewing," said Mamá.

Papi looked pleased. Maria looked at both of them. It hardly seemed like punishment.

"Well, Maria?" Papi said.

"Yes. Of course I will. That's fine," Maria said hastily.

"You will have to do as Mamá tells you," said Papi, as if this were something new.

"She can learn," said Mamá.

"But Mamá—" She hardly dared to ask. "I can still play ball?"

"That is up to your father," Mamá said.

Papi nodded. "This time. But any more fighting—"

"There won't be any more," Maria promised.

That night, when the world was still, Maria lay in her bed and tossed and tumbled. The problem was her mind. Her mind got up and roamed through the landscape of the whole previous day, weaving through all the things that had happened, refusing to let her sleep. She spent the night wide awake and only managed to sink into sleep for an hour or two.

The fine-feathered rooster woke her when he let loose the morning's first *kikiriki*!

Maria sat up, her heart racing. She knew what she could sew. A dress for Janie's sister. So she could go to graduation. She would talk to Mamá and she would learn to sew that dress.

Maria waited until Mamá woke up and went to get the eggs from the chicken coop and Papi went out to the bathhouse.

Then she crept down to the corner of the kitchen that was Mamá's sewing place. She pulled out the folds of cloth that Doña Elena had given her mother to make graduation dresses for customers. Here was a whole bolt of creamy ivory! Surely there was enough in it for one extra dress.

Fascinated by the silky fabric, she rolled it out, playing it over her own arm. She pulled it up to her neck and watched it run down her body. She held it up against the wooden doorframe where Papi had made notches for their height, hers and Emilio's. She tried to estimate how much Gloria topped her in height. A little bit, maybe a couple of inches. The vision of a silken dress danced in Maria's mind.

"Maria!"

Maria dropped the bolt, which nearly fell on her foot. "What are you doing?" Mamá grabbed the cloth and began to roll it up again, protecting it from the floor as best she could.

Maria found her voice. "Mami, it's Janie's sister!"

"What?" Mamá cried in exasperation. "What about Janie's sister? Go on, tell me. I'm listening, see? I want to understand. So tell me so I'm gonna understand." She flipped the end of the cloth onto the roll and put it back in its corner, brushing off a last speck of dust.

Maria told her all about Janie and her sister, Gloria, and how Janie's mamá cried all the time and wanted to run away to Mexico. How Gloria couldn't go to graduation because she didn't have a dress. How everything in their house was falling apart because their papa had died. How Elizabeth's nasty words were just the last blow to land on Janie, which was why Maria had leaped to her defense the day before.

She finished in a rush, "Mamá, it is so unfair! All I wanted to do was help! I thought, you have so much cloth, maybe we could use a little . . . I didn't mean to mess it up. . . ." She ground to a halt.

Mamá was speechless. She shook her head. For the longest time she just looked at Maria. Finally, she put her hand up to Maria's cheek, brushed a stray hair off it. She said, "All right. Let's see what we can do. Come with me."

Maria followed Mamá upstairs to the landing where she opened up the old steamer trunk. She took out the layers of cloth and the baby blanket. She lifted up the turbans and the papers that lay on top of them. She set them all on the ground. From the bottom of the trunk, she took out a couple of pieces of fabric. A pale yellow length of lace, another in pink.

"One of these, maybe," Mamá said. "What do you think?"

Maria said, "Mamá! That one." It lay beneath the others. It was not so much a piece of cloth as a cloud of soft, luscious peachy pink, the color of a sunrise shot through with strands of light. It was magical.

Mamá said, "Oh no, Maria. Papi bought this for me years ago. He said it reminded him of the cloth from his native land."

"Oh, well then," Maria said. "You should use it, Mamá."

"I never made it into anything," Mamá said. "I kept waiting for the right time. When you came along, I decided to keep it for you."

"For me?" cried Maria in shock.

"Of course for you," said Mamá. "Who else?"

Maria tried to imagine such a thing, herself in a dress made from that sunrise cloth. Maybe even a sari draped around her body the way she'd seen it in the family album, in a pale yellowing picture of Papi's own mother.

"Mamá," Maria said. "Why can't we use this to make the dress for Gloria?"

A small silence fell between them. "Are you sure?" Mamá said at last.

Why not? Maria thought. *Me? Never. Why, I'd probably rip it in two minutes flat.* She could not say that to Mamá, of course.

She said, "I am sure. It would make them all so happy."

Mamá nodded slowly. Then she smiled. She said, "M'ija, you have a good heart. Don't the saints tell us we must learn to be generous? I don't think Papi will mind. You can help me."

"You'd let me?" Maria reached out a finger and touched the cloth. It was satiny-smooth, like stroking a piece of heaven. "I can't sew so good," she said.

"You'll do your best," said Mamá in a tone that meant Maria could not dare do anything less.

CHAPTER TWENTY-ONE

One Short

JANIE WASN'T IN SCHOOL THAT DAY, BECAUSE she had to stay home and help her mother with a sick calf. When she did show up on Thursday, Maria hardly got to say two words to her. Finally, during multiplication tables, she managed to slip Janie a note.

We're making a dress for Gloria.

Between nine times seven and nine times nine, Janie whispered back to her across the aisle. "I know." Mamá had talked to Rosario Gill already.

"It's beautiful cloth," Maria said.

Janie smiled back, and Maria felt as good as if the dress were cut and sewed and ready. The rest of the day floated along on a kind of happy cloud, all the way to practice time. A few families had straggled in to watch—Ahmed Uncle had taken an early afternoon off from the restaurant and brought along the ik-do twins. Gramps Anderson was there as well, and an uncle of Lucy's who was visiting from Chico.

"Fielding," Miss Newman said. "We will work on fielding today."

"Where are the boys?" Dot asked.

"They were not invited this time," said Miss Newman. "They'll come back to help us out when we're ready for them." That was her only reference to the practice game that had ended in disaster, but it was enough.

Miss Newman had the girls work in pairs. In each round, one girl threw and one fielded. They threw grounders and fly balls alternately toward first and third base, so the girl who was fielding was constantly running back and forth, running, catching, turning, throwing. Lucy led off. She was so sure, she never once missed that ball.

Milly fooled her partner by making it look like it was a grounder coming, only then, lightning swift, there was the ball, flying high and making everyone laugh out loud. The girls all clapped when Sal and Joyce sped the drill up, faster and faster until they both fell in a heap from exhaustion! Everyone got sweaty and out of breath and it was purely wonderful.

There were the usual goatgrass burrs and the bumpy ground that made for erratic bouncing. None of it got anyone down.

Maria and Dot were partners. Their fly balls got wilder, so they had to end up sprinting almost to the fence to catch them. Miss Newman reined them in, but it was all good fun. At the end of their time, Dot threw the ball to the last pair—Connie and Elizabeth.

Elizabeth ripped out her first grounder. Connie fielded it, returned it, ran to catch the fly ball that followed. She missed. Another grounder, another fly. That one was too high, too wide. Missed again. Connie said nothing, just carried on. A few catches and then it was time to switch up.

Elizabeth caught Connie's first grounder. Caught it, returned it. Caught the fly ball. Returned it. Elizabeth ran back to first and missed the next one. "Hey!" she said. "What kind of pitching was that?"

"Sorry," Connie muttered. Maria didn't think it was a bad throw. It wasn't. It was fine.

Another round, another miss. "You did that on purpose," Elizabeth said.

"Now, then," said Miss Newman, touching her whistle cautiously as if she thought she might need to use it. She didn't, but the drill petered out after another few throws.

Practice continued. Position plays and then some work on line drives and communication. But Maria felt her spirits slumping.

At the end of practice, Miss Newman had news. "On the eighth of May," she said, "the county board will meet to decide on public projects for the second half of this year. Some of us have petitioned for the ball field to be put back on the agenda. You all should come."

Questions erupted. "Us?" "We're allowed?" "Will they let us talk?"

"You are most certainly allowed," Miss Newman said. "There will be a time for the public to speak up."

"Where's the meeting?" Lucy asked.

"At the county building in Yuba City."

"We're not old enough to vote!" said Janie's cousin Suze.

"That is true, but we still live in a democracy." When she meant business, Miss Newman always talked fancy. "So what do you think? Will you talk to your parents? Come. Let's make sure that our opinions are part of the public record."

"I'll come," Maria said. "I will."

"Me too," said Connie.

Janie said she'd be there too, so there it was, a pact between the three of them.

Others chimed in with questions. Miss Newman said, "I don't have all the answers. I have plenty of questions myself. But we should go and make ourselves heard."

Elizabeth said, "Not me."

"What?" said Maria.

"I said, 'Not me.' I won't be there," said Elizabeth.

"I see," said Miss Newman.

"Because," said Elizabeth, "I don't care about the ball field. I'm leaving anyway. We're moving to Sacramento by the end of the summer."

There was silence. "We'll be one short!" Joyce said.

It was true. There would be ten of them without Elizabeth. If something happened to any of them, they could not field a team.

And that was not all. At one time, Elizabeth's going away would have been great news. But now, knowing what it meant to Maria's family, it was nothing but bad news.

CHAPTER TWENTY-TWO

Still Home

ON FRIDAY THERE WAS NO PRACTICE AFTER SCHOOL. Papi picked Emilio and Maria up in his old red truck and took them to Anderson's Market and Feed Store.

"And how are you, my good man?" said Milly's grandfather.

"Fine, sir," said Papi in an extra-polite voice. *Because Gramps is Anglo,* Maria thought in surprise. She'd never noticed before how Papi spoke differently to white people. For some reason, it dismayed her.

Papi said Gramps Anderson was a man with a voice of thunder and a heart of gold. He was a little hard of hearing, so he often didn't wait for an answer but instead rolled right on with whatever he wanted to say. Gramps said, "I hear you girlies are going to be playing ball! A fine thing, if you ask me."

Maria grinned.

Emilio said, "Papi?" in his best pleading voice. "Can we get some Pep cereal?"

"You hate Pep cereal," Maria said.

"But I want the pins." So far, Emilio had one slightly rusty Pep pin with a Herby comic strip character on it. As always, he was alert to new collecting possibilities.

Papi said, "No, Son. No Pep."

Gramps said to Maria, "So, girlie? I hear you're handy with that ball. My Milly tells us you're all shaping up to be fine players."

"Is that right?" Papi looked surprised.

"Oh yes," said Gramps.

He picked a glass jar off a back shelf and pushed it across the counter to Maria. "Here, take some pickle juice to soak your hands in."

"What for?" said Papi, while Emilio opened his mouth into a puzzled O.

"Roughens them up good and proper, don't you know," said Gramps Anderson. "A player's gotta have some friction in his hands. Or her hands. Hey? How about that?" He grinned at Maria.

"Can I get something too?" said Emilio, tugging on the lick of hair on top of his head that wouldn't lie flat. "Like Pep?"

Gramps laughed out loud.

Papi pointed out the tub of butter mints to Emilio, who promptly forgot all about his Pep cereal and picked out a piece of the small round candy instead.

At the door, a figure in khaki coveralls stomped the dirt off his boots.

"Mr. Becker," Papi said, and once again his voice held caution and an extra layer of politeness. Mr. Becker nodded, all formal.

Gramps Anderson said, "Your daughter's playing too, right, Arnie? We'll see you at practice someday, maybe? Very good thing too, if I say so myself. You ought to get out a bit—a little relaxation. It'll do you a world of good."

Arnold Becker growled, "Nah. Too much to do." He plunked a five-dollar bill on the counter Lincoln side up, carelessly, as if to show everyone there was more where it came from. He yelled an order out—half a gallon of Purex and a pound package of noodles.

"Now, now, you don't have to shout," Gramps said, and pulled out a half package of flour instead of noodles. When Mr. Becker repeated his order in a normal voice, Gramps filled it correctly.

After Arnold Becker had gone, Gramps said, "The way that man frowns . . . I'm telling you, on an average day, I see more smiles right there across the road." He pointed in the direction of the funeral parlor owned by his son, Milly's papa.

"Speaking of which," said Gramps to Papi, "you got any more of those nice chrysanthemums?"

"Not this year," Papi said. He grew flowers for the funeral parlor every other year, so the soil got a chance to rest in between.

"Nobody's got a touch with mums like you do," said Gramps Anderson.

"It's nothing," Papi said modestly. "Chrysanthemums are only dressed-up marigolds."

"Say," said Gramps. "I hear that Arnie's going to sell and move away?"

Papi said that was true.

"Both lots together or is he dividing 'em up?" Gramps said. He meant the house and land the Beckers lived on and the smaller orchard and fields that Papi managed.

"Dividing," Papi said, as if he'd rather not say anything more on the subject.

"Well there you go. You ought to buy your place out from him." Gramps beamed as if he'd dreamed up the perfect solution.

Papi just shook his head.

"Why the devil not?" said Gramps in his usual blunt way. "You been working for Arnie for years. I'll bet you've got some money tucked away."

Papi said nothing.

"Well, time you owned the property instead of leasing. Something to pass on to the next generation, hey, Emilio?"

Hey, Emilio? Maria thought. *What about me? I'm next generation too.* She held her tongue.

Papi shuffled his feet. "Mr. Anderson, I wish I could," he said at last.

Gramps gave him a keen look. "That's a shame now," he said, "but I guess that's how it is." He didn't push the point further.

Papi ordered supplies from his list—a six-ounce jar of mustard, some vanilla, four cans of cleanser, and two dozen Mason lids and caps. He paid in a combination of money and ration stamps.

If I had the money, Maria thought, *and if a kid could do a thing like that, I would buy that land in a minute and give it to Papi for a birthday present.*

They said good-bye to Milly's grandpa and picked up their things. "I'll see you all someday at ball practice," Gramps said.

Much to Maria's surprise, Papi said, "Yes," and tipped his cap. Gramps nodded and got ready to greet the next family heading in to his store.

The truck waited in the dirt lot on Third Street, which fronted Anderson's, the barbershop, and the butcher on the corner. Papi opened the door. The children pulled themselves up into the cab. Papi rattled the engine awake.

Maria held fast to her jar of pickle juice.

"You're really going to soak your hands in that?" Papi demanded.

"I am." The liquid sloshed in the glass jar as the truck turned up the road and rumbled over the bridge.

"I never in my life heard of girls wanting rough hands,"

Papi said. "Your mamá gets her hands rough from all her work. I tell her to rub cream into them to soften them up, and here you want to soak your hands in salt water. What a strange world it is, my children."

He shook his head and smiled at Maria, as if she were an alien creature he did not understand but he loved her anyway. She grinned back at him. Emilio sucked noisily at the butter mint in his mouth and they drove on together.

CHAPTER TWENTY-THREE

Bright and Blessed

MARIA SOAKED HER HANDS IN THAT JAR OF BRINE until they reddened and wrinkled. The next morning, the tips of her fingers felt rougher. Were the palms tougher too or did she just imagine that?

As Maria helped Mamá knead dough to make flat Indian rotis for lunch, she felt pleased with her newly pickled hands. Before she pinched off the little balls of dough to roll them out on the counter, she took the entire wad and slapped it from hand to hand to make it smooth and elastic and stretchy, the way Mamá usually did.

"Muy bien," said Mamá in surprise, and handed her more dough.

Whack! Whup! Thwump! Maria threw the dough from one palm into the other as if she were throwing a ball. One.

Two. Three. Twenty throws later, Mamá had to rescue the dough from her daughter. "I have never seen you this enthusiastic about making tortillas before," said Mamá.

"Rotis. Tortillas. Tortis. Rotillas." Maria laughed.

"That's right," Mamá said. "Different and the same, all at once."

Mamá asked Maria about ball practice. Maria told her about fly balls and grounders, also different and the same. Mamá listened. She even smiled. It made the threats looming over their heads seem a little more distant than before.

Mamá listened to Maria telling her about the ball field and the meeting on the eighth of May. About Elizabeth saying she was moving to Sacramento—that last brought a little twist to Mamá's lip. Rolling out the Punjabi rotis—or maybe they were Mexican tortillas—Mamá said, "You do the best you can. That's all any of us can do."

If that sounded like a test, maybe it was, because after lunch, Mamá put Maria to work on Doña Elena's sewing.

"I thought we were going to do my shorts," Maria said.

"Patience," said Mamá.

Maria's patience was severely stressed. Mamá proceeded to sew as if a ghost had taken hold of her. "Pull that

185

thread out for me," she commanded. "Thread that bobbin. And that one. Pink on this, white on the other. Where are the stickpins?"

As the afternoon wore on, Mamá got more and more demanding. "I want you to keep an extra needle threaded every time I need it." "Iron that seam. Press it flat. You call that flat?"

And so on and on over the whir of the sewing machine. Maria's fingers were sore from getting stuck with needles. Even her hand that was hardened from throwing and catching balls started to ache from the dead weight of the solid, flat iron. She cleaned up discarded bits of fabric. She threaded bobbins for the old Singer machine. Her fingers got jabbed with the stickpins that held the seams together until Mamá could sew them into place. Maria's job was to pull the stickpins out as Mamá ran the seams on the machine, one at a time, joining sleeves to bodices and waists to skirts, running a silky swirl of cloth around each neckline to fall in front and tie together or bunch up in a rosette at the shoulder. Maria's back hurt from bending over the cloth, and she grew cross-eyed from the dazzle of it in her eyes, hour after hour.

But slowly, slowly, over the course of the day, flouncy

shapes and slinky shapes began to appear. In ivory and rose, misty blue and mauve, they shimmered into being, and every ache and soreness in Maria's body was given to them in penitence. The most beautiful one of all was a marvel of sunshine-colored silk, with cap sleeves and buttons running down at a slant from shoulder to waist.

The best was yet to come. At the end of the day, Mamá pulled a pattern out from underneath her pile. "Look what I found last time I was at Doña Elena's."

"Oh Mami, Mami!" Maria threw herself at her mother. "My shorts!"

The pattern was for a grown woman, but Mamá could adjust it down to Maria's size. The top was a bit too fancy, but Mamá said she could make it plainer. Suddenly Maria's aching fingers were ready to cut and pin and thread all over again.

That Sunday after church, the little mountain range that everyone called Los Picachos came alive to music. The uncles sang. Papi had brought his precious drum, wrapped carefully in its padded cloth covering.

Gloria's dress was handed over, wrapped in brown paper and accompanied by much hugging and a few happy sniffles. Maria told Connie about the shorts that were all sewed and ironed and ready to wear now.

"You just keep my old ones for a backup," Connie said.

"Thank you," Maria said. "I will." Two weeks ago, Maria would have given them back. She would not have understood why Connie should be hurt by that. Now she was simply thankful.

News had spread as well of the county board meeting in Yuba City on the eighth of May. Tim Singh's father raised it with the men. "You're going, no? My Timmo told us."

"It's for the kids," most of the men said. "Of course we must go."

Boys and girls together, the kids chimed in about that meeting, how they'd never build the ball field if the kids and their families did not attend and make their views heard.

"Miss Newman said we must speak up," Maria said.

"Because that's how democracy works!" Connie added.

"Ahmed," Papi said to Connie's dad. "Are you taking Consuelo?" Papi always called Connie by her proper given name.

Ahmed Uncle nodded. "Taking all the kids. We're making an outing of it."

It was what Papi didn't say that surprised Maria. He

didn't say the families should be quiet and not stick their necks out. He didn't say the county board had power and they did not.

Instead he chucked Maria under the chin and said, "You want to go? This field—this game—it's so important to you?"

"Yes, Papi." She waited for a long moment.

"I'll take you," said Papi at last. "I have never been to one of those meetings before."

"Anyone can go, really," Maria said. "They are open meetings."

Papi snorted. "But not everyone can vote for those people on the board. They are happy to take my taxes, but they will not let me vote." The uncles nodded. They knew how democracy worked, how some people were allowed to be a part of it and others were not. Still, they agreed, the public was invited and they were part of the public.

With all the troubles in the world, on this bright and blessed day, there was also dancing. The men laughed and clapped their hands and described circles around the women and children.

Mamá and the aunties rocked and clapped, and slowly, slowly, a few of them got up to dance. And if the toss of their hair and the swish of their skirts was more Mexico than Punjab, more flamenco than bhangra, no one really cared, the children least of all. They ran headlong into the stomping and circling, following this step here and that one there, making up patterns of their own in the warmth of the day.

Stomp-stomp, clap-clap-clap, snap of the fingers, and turn-turn-turn! The children raised their arms in the air the way Papi and the uncles did. They shouted, "Hai!" and "Ballay, ballay!" smack on the notes at the end of each vibrating verse, following the upswing of the men's voices.

The music awakened a wild girl in Maria. Bending her arms at the elbow like the uncles, lifting her hands over her head and twirling them at the wrists, she matched their steps. She whirled like a top. She flung herself into the rhythms so they played up and down her legs, the drumbeats thrumming in her bones, sending little thrills into her face and her arms.

This was an old, old dance that Papi and the uncles had brought with them when they came to California from their homeland in India. *They are remembering those old times when they dance,* Maria realized, *the way Papi remembers when he tells us stories.* Only a week ago she might have been impatient. She might have thought, *What is the use of always remembering when that time is long gone?* But now Papi had said he didn't want to tell stories anymore, and Maria wondered, *Does it hurt to remember?* All the adha-adha families seemed to carry such memories, tender and beautiful and painful all at once.

"Ballay, ballay!" Ahmed Uncle cried, and the final stomps and snapping of fingers brought the bhangra to its end.

"Maria!" said Papi, pinching her cheek as if she were still a baby. "Come. Come and sit with your old papi." He sat down on one of the boulders that served quite well for seats. He patted the place next to him. He wiped his forehead with his handkerchief.

Maria sat, breathless, on the warm rock.

"You have grown so big," Papi said.

Maria nodded.

"Mamá tells me you helped her sew a dress for Gian's daughter," Papi said. "With the cloth from the trunk."

"Is that okay, Papi? Mamá said you wouldn't mind."

"It is wonderful," Papi said.

Maria was suddenly tongue-tied.

"Your friends are also playing ball? Janie. Consuelo."

Papi made a gesture of throwing a ball into the air. A clumsy throw, like someone unused to it.

"Yes, Papi. Look. Like this." Maria stood up, took a stance, and threw a swift imaginary pitch. "Oh Papi! You'll see. It's so much fun." She hugged him hard, making him break into pretend grumbles in Punjabi. She didn't understand the words, but she loved the sound of them anyway.

CHAPTER TWENTY-FOUR

The Ugly Truth

PRACTICE WAS CANCELED ON MONDAY ON ACCOUNT of Miss Newman's going to Sacramento to visit her sick mother. Maria roamed around the house, tossing her old ball from one hand to the other, until she strayed dangerously close to the kitchen altar and Mamá said, "Go outside and play."

Maria fled outdoors, with Emilio tailing her like a shadow. "Play with me, Maria, play with me."

"All right. I'll pitch and you bat."

Armed with the ball and an old dime-store bat, they set off. Emilio's batting was on the wild side. Maria had to field the ball in the ditch and among the thistles.

Smack! Thud! She ran down the road, away from their little house, chasing that ball until it landed close to the big farmhouse fence. "Boy, you got a strong arm, Emilio," she said. "Take it easy."

Beyond the fence lay the Beckers' house.

Whack! Whack! Closer and closer. It drew her like a magnet, that house. She tried not to look at it, but there it was, and the man inside had all the power. She should run in the other direction. Emilio would follow if she did.

She didn't run.

His next swing thwacked the ball right over the fence.

"Oh, Emilio!" Maria looked around her. The day was silent but for the red-winged blackbirds swishing their way between the trees.

Quickly she scaled the fence, finding the ball at last in a prickly weed patch. She stopped. Still no one around. She retrieved it, pulled a goatgrass sticker off her hand, and climbed back over. "Not that way, Emilio," she warned him. "Hit it the other way."

She threw the ball, and felt something give in her shoulder. Too late, she remembered she should be careful with that shoulder.

She'd meant to run after the ball. Meant Emilio to hit it away from the house. Away. Away.

Emilio smacked the ball as hard as he could. It flew

wild and wide and far, and in the worst possible direction.

Glass shards tinkled.

"Emilio!" Maria groaned. "What a stupid thing to do. Didn't I tell you?"

"I didn't . . ." Emilio began.

"Yes, you did too. I never would have come this far except for your dumb batting."

Emilio's mouth drooped. "I didn't mean . . ." he began.

"Oh, shut it, 'Milio," she said, all her recent resolutions taking flight like so many blackbirds. "Get lost!"

She launched herself over the fence once more, ignoring the wrench in her shoulder, and leaving her brother blinking after her through the railings. She ran up to the window and began to look for the ball.

It wasn't anywhere among the weeds, or in the untended flower beds. Of course not. When it broke the glass, it must have flown way inside. She turned in a panic.

She wasn't fast enough. A loud voice shouted, "Hey! Hey you! Come here!"

Maria turned. Run! said her mind. But her feet stayed put.

"You?" said Mr. Becker. "Again?"

Once more that shameful feeling clutched at Maria.

Only this time it was earned. She had no business being here.

She said, "We were just playing."

"We?"

"I." Maria didn't dare turn to see if Emilio was still there. "I was playing," she said.

"Damnit, girl!"

"I'm sorry," said Maria, and made herself add, "sir." The silver edge of shattered glass caught the light.

"I-I'll pay for it." Maria thought briefly of the jar of coins under her bed. How much did a windowpane cost?

"You'll pay for it!" He laughed out loud. Maria flinched. *Papi's gonna belt me now, and I'll deserve it, she thought. I should have stopped Emilio. I shouldn't have thrown him the ball when I knew he was hitting it all over the place.* The shoulds and shouldn'ts bounced around in her mind—if only, if only, reminders of good intentions gone badly wrong.

"Come on." Mr. Becker clamped a heavy hand on her elbow and marched her up the front steps. "Come see what you've done." Up the steps and into the house. Into the house! Maria never in a hundred years would have thought she'd be standing there in the Beckers' kitchen, looking at a scattering of broken glass. It looked like an ordinary kitchen. A gas stove, an oven, a meat safe, a drying rack. No gun racks in sight.

"Should I . . . clean it up?" She didn't dare look him in the face.

"Go ahead." He pointed to a broom and dustpan in the corner.

Swallowing hard, Maria started to sweep up the silver daggers from the floor. She peeked around her. A picture of a woman sat on a cupboard against the back wall. A pretty woman with Elizabeth's eyes, if you could put a smile into Elizabeth's eyes.

"What are you staring at?" said Mr. Becker.

"Nothing." Maria carried on sweeping until all the little bits of glass were in the pan. It took an age.

He handed her a sheet of newspaper, and she emptied the glass into it and folded it over carefully, hoping she wouldn't cut herself.

Then she waited. He said, "I'll be talking to your daddy about this, so don't go running to him with a pack of lies."

Maria gulped down her fear. She said nothing.

"Sorry bunch," he said. "Well, you'll be out of here soon enough."

Something about the hardening of his face should have scared Maria witless. Instead it swept her fear away, swept it into the corners of that uncared-for kitchen where cobwebs hung from the wooden rafters; sent it flying onto the top of the icebox, its surface coated with a fine sheen of dust. She blurted out, "What is that supposed to mean?"

Becker jerked his head up and stared at her.

The floodgates of Maria's hurting heart had opened now. "You're planning to throw us out, just like that? What did we ever do to you? What did my papi ever do?" The words came pouring out of her and they were true, true, true, every last one. "He'd buy the land off you if he could, but he can't, can he, because the law won't let him, and you know that!"

He stared at her with his pale, unreadable eyes. "Funny little creature, aren't you?" he said. "Does your daddy know you're out here speaking up for him?"

Maria said nothing.

"Well, does he?"

"Never mind," she said. What a mocking, cruel man! "You're not going to listen to me, anyway. Everyone knows—" She stopped, knowing she'd crossed a thin line between daring and foolishness.

"What?" he demanded. "Everyone knows what?"

"Nothing," muttered Maria. "May I go home now?"

Mr. Becker walked across the room, and stood in the doorway. He blocked her way out, his arms folded across his chest. "What does everyone know? That my granddad and grandma were German? It's not exactly a state secret."

He held the ball out to her. Maria felt her knees weaken. Gathering her courage, she took it from his hand and checked it for glass shards.

Papi had said, Keep your eye on the truth. What would happen if she told the truth now? She whispered, and somehow the picture of the woman on the cupboard gave her courage. "No, I didn't mean that. I meant— what people say. You been different since—since your wife died. Angry or something. Angry at everyone." It was all truth, so why did it sound so ugly when she spoke it out loud?

The big man in front of her clenched his fists so tightly that the knuckles showed bone-white under his skin.

"Even at your daughter," Maria said.

Mr. Becker took a step toward her and Maria thought, *He's going to kill me and bury me under the steps and I'll never see Mamá and Papi and Emilio again.*

But Arnold Becker seemed to change his mind. He went back to the kitchen table and sat heavily back down. All he said, waving her toward the door, was, "You tell your father I'll be talking to him."

"Yes, sir," said Maria, and fled, her heart chugging like an express train.

Her right hand stung. As she let herself out the front gate, she rubbed it with the palm of her left hand to make it better. Where was Emilio? He'd probably run on home. Just as well.

"What's this I hear?" Mamá demanded when Maria scraped the mud off her shoes and came in the house.

"Where's Emilio?" Maria said.

"He came home," said Mamá. "He told me about a broken window."

"Mami!" Maria cried, and the whole sorry tale came tumbling from her. "And I swept it up, and I swear I thought he was going to kill me, but he didn't and oh, Mamá, I yelled at Emilio, I did, and I am so, so sorry!"

There was silence.

"He's going to throw us out anyway," Mamá said softly, as if she were speaking to herself.

Maria started to say I'm sorry once again, but it sounded stupid and useless so she didn't.

Finally Mamá said, "Maria, I'm going to lie down for a while. My head hurts."

Maria nodded miserably. Her hand was all grubby. A little blood had oozed into the middle of her palm and streaked the lines on it a blotchy red. A glass piece must have worked its way under the skin without her noticing it. She rubbed at it but it only itched more.

Mamá's face had never looked this way before. So fearful.

CHAPTER TWENTY-FIVE

Hate

MARIA SHOULD HAVE READ THE SIGNS. SHE SHOULD have read the signs the following day at practice, but she did not.

"I can't wait," Elizabeth was saying to anyone who would listen. "I just can't wait to be out of this deadbeat town. Did I tell you we're heading for Sacramento? Did I tell you?" And she gave Maria a sideways, sneering look.

Some of the girls were curious. They wanted to know about Sacramento and when was she moving. "Just as soon as my dad's done with his business commitments, that's when," Elizabeth told them. "I can't tell you how much I am longing to leave. This town is just—oh, it's just—despicable." Her voice had a hard, careful edge.

A few of the girls exchanged looks but said nothing.

"My dad's going to be investing in a new radio station in Sacramento," Elizabeth said. "Maybe they'll let me get a foot in the door too. I could help out around the station, learn a few things about radio announcing, who knows?"

Dot turned to Maria and Connie. "Come on. Race you?" The three of them ran across the field to the fence. They hoisted themselves up and perched on top, their legs swinging. "That Elizabeth," Dot muttered. "What a show-off."

"Some people are nasty to her daddy," Connie said unexpectedly. Maria stared at her. Why was Connie taking Elizabeth's side?

"He's not always mean," Connie said. "I think sometimes he's all right. And I heard they had a broken window yesterday."

Maria froze. She wanted to tell Connie and Dot what had happened. That it was a mistake, it wasn't nastiness. She'd meant to tell Connie during the day but somehow she couldn't bring herself to. Now there was no time, and Miss Newman was hurrying up to call them to their drills, so she had to let it be.

"Infield practice today," Miss Newman said. "Didi, ready to step up? Grab a bat. Connie, you pitch."

Didi and Connie got to their places.

"Elizabeth—third base. Maria—shortstop. Janie—first, Lucy—second! Go, go, go!"

Elizabeth had better not try to hog that ball.

The ball flew out, with a little bend on it. "Good pitch, Connie!"

Didi managed to hit it—smack! She took off running.

Maria steadied herself. There it was, heading her way, between third base and shortstop. She could field it, but so could Elizabeth. It was a judgment call.

Elizabeth fielded it cleanly but then when she threw it, it was a nothing throw; no effort in it at all.

The ball thumped onto the ground far short of the base, so that Janie had to race forward practically six feet. What was Elizabeth thinking? She wasn't, that was the answer. Her mind was already in Sacramento. Or maybe on that window with its glass that had shattered into so many daggers.

Elizabeth gone. That meant no more thorn in her side, that was for sure. But it also meant that they would have to leave. And go where? Maria shook that other terrible thought out of her mind. She couldn't think of what it meant. Not now.

Janie grabbed the ball. She whipped around to try to tag the runner, but it was too late. Didi made it to first base, waving her hands in the air.

"I could have fielded that," Maria said.

"Yeah?" said Elizabeth.

"Yeah," said Maria.

"Now then, girls," said Miss Newman.

It wasn't over.

"Batting practice," said Miss Newman. "Elizabeth, let's see you pitch. Lucy, you're catcher."

That worked, under Lucy's sharp eye and swift arm. At least until it was Maria's turn to bat. "I'm going to whiz it way past you," Elizabeth called. "You won't even see it coming."

"Oh yeah?" Maria called back. That sounded better. Just talk, the kind of talk the girls always did among themselves? "Pop it up for me!" she called.

Elizabeth grasped the ball, one foot on the makeshift wooden pitcher's plate. She stepped out, wound up, and let . . . it . . . fly.

Maria stood in batting stance, feet shoulder-width apart, held her bat high, ready to step in to smack that ball. She squinted, keeping up with the pitch. There it came.

Maria swung with all her might—in her mind she'd hit

it already. But reality was not her mind, and whoosh! She spun around. She hadn't connected.

"Eye on the ball," said Miss Newman. "Don't swing too soon."

"What a breeze that was," said Elizabeth. "Hey, thanks, Maria—I needed to cool off."

Maria tried to make sense of it. Elizabeth never joshed around like that with the others. Still, so what? Maria tried to keep her eye on the ball but something distracted her. Someone was walking along the fence, coming up to the dirt field, stopping to watch the girls practice. Papi? But there wasn't the time. She forced herself not to look that way.

The next pitch was too low and outside—far outside. She didn't even swing. The catcher upped and ran for the ball.

Maria prayed that the next pitch would be clean. "Get it over the plate," she muttered. Something was wrong. What was Elizabeth up to?

By the third pitch, Elizabeth was glaring daggers at Maria. Connie, now at second base, was shifting uneasily from foot to foot.

Elizabeth planted her feet together, ball in both hands. Then she lifted her left leg, reeled back, stretched, and—what was she doing? Pitching was supposed to be underhand. Elizabeth squinted her eyes.

"Elizabeth," said Miss Newman. Even that did not stop her.

And then Maria got it. Hadn't she gotten it wrong on their very first practice? Hadn't she tried to show them all how Babe Ruth had coached the girls on the newsreel? It was all in fun, but now Elizabeth was mocking her!

"Take that!" Elizabeth yelled, and then she let fly.

Maria turned cold. That ball—

Someone yelled, "Look out!" in a funny, broken-up voice.

Too late. The ball cracked her in the head. Miss Newman's whistle blew and blew.

A voice shouted in Punjabi. Maria tried to say *Papi!* before she dropped like a stone.

She awoke to a row of blurry faces peering down at her, Papi cradling her head in his hands and Miss Newman pressing a cold towel to the side of her face. She thought, *Why does my head feel like it's burst into a million pieces?*

She blinked at the faces and they came into focus, but slowly, as if her eyes had trouble working. Why couldn't she see properly? Panic clutched at her, but she couldn't move, couldn't speak, couldn't do anything.

Miss Newman said, "Maria, can you talk? Can you hear me?" And Papi—why, Papi was crying.

Maria tried to get up, but her muscles wouldn't cooperate. The ache in her head turned her stomach queasy. She tried to say, *Papi, I'm okay,* but it came out all strangled.

"Don't you move now," said Miss Newman. "Stay still, you hear me? I'll go right away to get help."

Maria tried to speak again but still no words would come and the pain—the pain! It was so very strong. She'd never felt pain like that before. Was that her forehead that was swelling over her left eye now so she could not see? Panic overcame her, waves of it.

Miss Newman hesitated for one moment, almost as if she might have been waiting for a killer ball to come whizzing out of nowhere. Then she said all in a rush, "You all stay right here, and you do not let that girl move. I'm going inside to phone for an ambulance."

The ambulance ride was a blur of noise, but Papi was there with her. He would be there always and that helped to calm Maria down.

At Yuba City Hospital, a nurse in a starched white cap and pinafore took Maria's temperature and pulse, listened to her heart, and told her to sit still. Another nurse came along after a while and made her stick her tongue out. She tapped Maria on the knee and elbow, examined the bruise on her forehead and told her it was looking good. It did not feel in the least good, but since Papi said he would personally hold Maria still if she did not quit wriggling, she gave up. When the doctor arrived to look at her, he said he wanted to be sure that she was not brain-injured, only mildly concussed. After four hours of observation, they finally let her go home.

All of this gave Maria plenty of thinking time to reflect upon what it was she'd seen in Elizabeth's face and how she had invited this blow upon herself. Through the pain, Maria knew what she should have seen but had not. Elizabeth's grandstanding should have tipped her off. That was the sign she had read all wrong. She'd read it through her own guilt. She'd read it as pride. It was so much more than that. It was hate.

Everyone had some hate in them these days. Everyone was a little crazed from it—from Janie's dad dying and the war. From knowing that the Germans were bad people, so you were supposed to hate them. But then what about Elizabeth and her dad? You could get filled with hate from all the calling of names—all the times the adha-adha kids got called "dirty Indian" and "half and half" and got told to "go back where you came from!" And so of course it seemed to Elizabeth that Maria had broken that window out of hate as well, when that was simply not true.

When you are angry to start with, if someone gives you a person to hate, then you hate him because it feels better than burning it all up inside you. There was Becker with his German name right there, ready to be hated. It was mad, mad, mad. This war made too many people in this country hate each other. Now Maria knew why Mamá was afraid when Emilio got in fights. The stirring together of all these notions in her mind made her head throb so violently she thought she would throw up. All of Elizabeth's pretend happiness about moving to Sacramento was just that. Underneath it all was hate.

CHAPTER TWENTY-SIX

Not Fast Enough

ADOLF HITLER WAS DEAD. THAT WAS WHAT THEY said on the radio on Wednesday. Maria thought his death should have meant the war was over, but that was not so. It was still going on in the Pacific and people were still dying, even in Europe. From the crackle of the news on the radio, there was no break in the fighting.

Maria had been moved temporarily into her parents' bedroom, so she would have a real bed to lie on and a door that could be closed to keep Emilio out. Mamá and Papi slept on Maria's pile of mattresses. With each day, Maria discovered new bruises blooming on her—on her hip and on her shoulder.

Another of Tía Manuela's postcards had arrived. A

picture of Redondo Drive, home of the stars in Hollywood. She'd written:

Hope to come home for a quick break soon.

Keep smiling (Maria this means you).

Emilio, can't wait to see how much you've grown.

    Love, Manuela.

Maria had to stay in bed, according to the home visit nurse. "No complaints, Missy," said Nurse Ballard. "You stay put." She added something about lesions and reflexes, shone a light in Maria's eye, and seemed satisfied. She left severe instructions—rest and more rest. No break there.

Once, when Maria turned over in bed, the muscles in her shoulder complained. "What's the matter?" asked Mamá, who guarded her like a lioness.

Maria shook her head. Maybe it would go away. It was just a soreness from when she fell. She must have fallen on that side—she could not remember. She favored the shoulder, tried not to put any weight on it. She couldn't lift anything.

Even Emilio wasn't allowed to come in for a chat, threatened with losing all chances of getting his precious blue stamp if he disobeyed.

If she'd only seen the ball coming quicker, Maria could

have moved faster. It might have whizzed right past her head then.

All the time the news on the radio went on and on about Hitler. Something about a bunker in Berlin and a woman that Hitler had married only the day before he died, and the bodies were buried quickly.

What did all this mean for the war? Well, the German Army had surrendered in Italy. Didn't surrender mean it was all over? Apparently not.

While the radio blared out the latest news from the European Front, Maria had plenty of time to think. Papi was listening all the time to the war stuff on the radio. He too seemed to be thinking a lot.

Papi often said, "What's the use of saying 'If only?' Once the locusts have eaten up your crop, it's useless to wish you'd harvested it earlier." But now, with all his dreaming about a free India and changes in American law, Papi himself seemed to be living in the land of "If only . . ." Every time he came up to see Maria he wore a frown.

"Free world, free world," Papi said. "They are all talking about the free world, but India is still not free." Papi said India was supposed to be free by now. After that, the laws in the United States of America were supposed to change, so that people from India like Papi and the uncles could be allowed to become citizens. "If they would listen to us, they would understand," said Papi. "We should have been stronger. We should have made them listen." He talked to Maria, but sometimes he talked past her to the whole wide world where nobody was listening.

The world was not moving fast enough, Papi said. The world was just not moving fast enough.

Maria's lips were dry and the medicine left her with an unpleasant taste in her mouth. She listened to Papi and licked her lips, trying to dispel the bitterness. She tried to remember the old Papi she knew, before the frown became so deeply engraved upon his face.

Once, when Emilio was a baby, Papi had taken them on a long, long driving trip, all the way to San Francisco. They'd wrapped the baby in a blanket till only his face showed with his little snotty nose. You had to keep on wiping it so he didn't mess up his blanket. His shiny black eyes darted everywhere, taking in the world so new for him, so shiny new and full of secrets. Maria had held him on her lap for a while until he got too fussy and then Mamá took him back. They walked by the bay and breathed in the cool sea air.

Maria remembered only three things about that trip.

Emilio bouncing, the air on her skin, and her lips on the drive back home. How dry they were, and with new tastes, of fish and seaweed and salt. She licked them often afterward and was sad to find out that the new tastes went away.

Now there was only the taste of bitter medicine.

That night Papi came thumping up the steps and into the room, and sat down on the bed. "Maria," he said. "Your Mamá and I have been talking. We think it's best that you don't play ball for a while now."

"What?" Maria cried, sitting bolt upright and making an explosion of pain burst through her head so she had to fall back with a groan.

"Look," said Papi. "You must give yourself time to heal."

"Papi . . ." Maria started, but she felt so purely bad that she couldn't carry on.

"I saw what happened, my girl," he said, and the tears swam in his eyes. "It was so horrible. I don't know why you want to play such a game."

Maria tried to say that it wasn't the game, it was just crazy Elizabeth. She wanted to say that she knew Papi loved her but he was all wrong. All wrong, could he not see that? A tear trickled out of Maria's eye. Despite her furious blinking—*no llores, no llores!*—it wouldn't obey.

Papi brought out his big handkerchief and gave it to her. She dabbed at her eyes, blew her nose, and clutched the soft cloth tightly.

Then, to her astonishment, Papi pulled out his sharp steel kirpan from where he always carried it, tucked into his belt.

He said, "There, don't cry."

She watched in amazement as he pulled the little knife out of its case and put it flat side against her head. He held it there until she sensed herself grow still. She felt its metal upon her skin, cold and heavy. Then Papi lifted it off and set it down on the bed by her pillow. He said, "This knife will give you strength."

It would? Papi's eyes held stories about this, she had a feeling, but of course he wasn't going to tell them, was he? She needed strength now, more than anything.

"We must face reality," Papi said, "even if it makes us feel bad." And what reality did he mean—the reality of no more playing ball? That made Maria cry even harder because it made her think, and she did not want to think about reality at that moment.

Reality was scary, like having to leave home. Like feeling

hot and bothered inside from things that other people said and did. The way Mr. Becker looked at them. Reality was admitting to being sad for Janie and now feeling something unnameable for Elizabeth. Just thinking of it gave her a funny jolt in the pit of her stomach.

Reality was not knowing how she could tell Papi. Tell him not to be afraid for her, not to stop her from doing the one thing she really wanted to do. It was about telling the truth and not making up things because you wanted them that way.

Papi was right. You had to have courage to look the truth in the eye. Bumps on the head were easy in comparison.

She gave Papi back his handkerchief. He folded it and put it carefully into his pocket, even though she'd sniffled all over it and blown her nose in it even.

Papi began to sing softly. It was an old Punjabi prayer that Maria didn't fully understand, but as he sang, the knots inside her loosened up a little, and she found herself sinking, sinking into stillness.

His singing faded into murmurs. He tucked the kirpan once again into his belt where it belonged. He said, "Don't be afraid. God will provide." Maria hoped he was right, but it was a frail kind of hoping.

CHAPTER TWENTY-SEVEN

A Frail and Slender Hope

AS SOON AS SHE WAS AWAKE THE FOLLOWING DAY, even though she could barely raise her head from the pillow, Maria tried to engage Mamá in a debate about the new and unpleasant truth of no more playing ball for the whole season—what was the point of all the practice, then? What was the point of sewing those shorts? But Mamá was having none of it and Maria didn't have the energy to try too hard.

All Mamá would say was, "¡Silencio, Maria! You need to rest. No more talk."

But perhaps Papi's God was working overtime after all, because a couple of days later a trickle of children came calling. By the afternoon the trickle had turned into a flood.

Janie and her sister and a couple of their older cousins came to visit, with the news that Gloria's new dress fit like a charm.

Lucy and Dot and some of their friends from Marysville came too. Lucy said the boys had come back to help with practice. The girls had struck out the boys' best batters. It was all going great, but everyone missed Maria.

Milly came and so did her big brother Matthias and her little sister Molly. Sal and Joyce and all of their brothers showed up; that was half a dozen right there.

Tim and Mondo and their friend Charley and Charley's friends Bill and Pete.

Even Joey Hamilton from down the road, and his sister Susan. Had Maria even known that Joey had a sister?

"You're having a party?" said the home visit nurse, when Mamá let her in to check on Maria. "My patient must be feeling better." She had a time getting the guests to be silent so that she could take her patient's pulse, not to mention hear herself think.

But the hordes were not here just to see Maria. They were on a mission, and Connie was their leader. "Is Maria well enough? To come with us to the board meeting in Yuba City?" Connie asked.

"Not today," said the nurse, alarmed.

A dozen voices assured her. "Not today!" "Next week!" "Tuesday, the eighth!" "Can she go?" "Please!"

"I don't know about that . . ." Mamá began, but the nurse said briskly, "The doctor will see her first thing Monday. I predict she'll be good as gold in a couple of days."

"Really?" said Mamá.

"Mamá!" Maria nearly sprang up in delight.

The nurse pushed her back down. "Not so fast."

"Really?" cried Maria. "Can I go?"

"Unless Dr. Duncan forbids it," said the nurse. "He has final say-so, naturally. I'll check with him, shall I?"

"Yes, *please*," Maria begged.

Mamá tapped her fingers thoughtfully on the nightstand before seeing the nurse to the door.

A pandemonium of delight broke out. The hope that had seemed so frail and slender the night took sudden flight and soared. If the doctor said yes . . . .

Mamá shooed all the kids out except for Connie.

"The doctor's going to let you," Connie said. "I'm sure he will."

Maria nodded. If the doctor agreed, then Mamá would help her convince Papi that she should go. Maria was sure she would. *Permission,* she thought. *There's always someone you have to get permission from when you are a kid.*

Connie said, "I got some more news for you."

"What?"

"You know my glove?"

"Your lefty glove."

"Yup. Well, guess who it came from?"

"Miss Newman?"

"No, no. I mean yes, but guess who donated it."

"I don't know. Who?"

"Guess."

"Milly's gramps? Mr. Walker? I don't know. Just tell me."

Connie leaned over and whispered in Maria's ear.

"The old—I mean, Mr. Becker? You can't mean that. How do you know?"

"Elizabeth told me. Miss Newman asked everyone in town, and Mr. Becker had his old glove from when he was a boy, and he's a lefty, so there. That's why it's so old, but it fits. So what, right?"

"Right," Maria said, but her head spun. Just when you thought you'd figured things out, people turned around and stunned you with the things they did! Wow. Becker gave his old glove to the team? He cared enough? Somehow this bit of news shook everything up. Who was good and who was bad? Who was right and who was wrong, and how could you even tell?

One step, she decided, at a time. The first thing to do was get well and go to that meeting.

CHAPTER TWENTY-EIGHT

Board Meeting

AT FIRST, PAPI PUT UP A STRUGGLE. WAS MAMÁ sure Maria was well enough?

Of course she was sure. The doctor himself had said so, and the nurse had seconded the opinion—did Papi not trust these professional people?

No, no, of course he did. But could others not go and report back to Maria? He himself would do that if necessary. He seemed determined to keep Maria chained to the bed for her own good.

Mamá said she thought Maria was strong enough, well enough. *Mamá is an ally now, and when you have Mamá on your side,* Maria thought, *the saints themselves would have a tough battle against you.*

Papi was not sure how much good the meeting would

do, anyway. These things were all decided by people in those stuffy boardrooms, he declared. Did they really care what the public thought?

Maria pleaded. "Papi, please. You did promise you'd take me. Way back. Remember?"

Keeping his word mattered to Papi. It mattered above all else. Papi and the uncles were all very clear on that. You couldn't make a promise and then not keep it. Maybe Papi remembered his own words to Maria as well, back in the churchyard at the Iglesia de Santa Rosa.

Anyone can go, Maria had said to Papi. *They are open meetings.* And Papi had said in reply, *But not everyone can vote for those people on the board.*

Neither Papi nor Maria could vote, it was true. But maybe, after all, Papi had decided to give his daughter a chance to change the minds of the powerful people on that board.

Papi kept his word. He cranked up the truck and piled children in—not only Maria, but also Emilio, Janie, Connie, and assorted Khan brothers and sisters.

When they chugged into town, they had to park on a dirt embankment down by the bridge, because the entire length of Second Street in front of the county courthouse was jammed full of cars and trucks that had gotten there before them.

Miss Newman said, "I'm glad to see you, Maria. Are you all healed now?" She cast an anxious glance at Maria's forehead, where the purple bruise was still visible.

"I think so . . ." Maria started to say but just then Miss Newman spotted Papi. "Oh heavens," she cried. "I'm forgetting myself. I'm so glad you're here, Mr. Singh." She held out her hand, gripped Papi's, and said, "Your girl is a natural on the ball field. I hope to see her back soon. Isn't it a fine thing for our young girls to learn to play team sports?"

Papi got that wary, polite look on his face, the one he always got when he was dealing with Anglo people. But before he could say a word in reply, as if there couldn't possibly be another opinion on the subject, Miss Newman waved them all into the packed meeting room, where the board of supervisors were even now getting seated at their long polished desk up on the dais. There were five of them behind that desk. They all looked very important with their suits and ties. The man in the middle held a gavel, and every now and then he would bang on the desk with it. Even the gavel was decorated with a little band of shiny brass on its hammering end.

"All rise," said the clerk.

Papi whipped his cap off and bowed his head. Even the newspaper reporter from the *Appeal-Democrat* put his pencil and notepad away.

Next came the pledge to the flag. Maria recited it, hand on heart, hearing her voice join with everyone else's. ". . . one nation, indivisible, with liberty and justice for all." It felt like a celebration.

The board got down to business with a lot of banging of the gavel and motioning to order. The men at the high desk began to talk about grading the road to the migrant workers' housing on Garden Highway, and about the new peach strain that the Harters were working on developing in their family orchards.

A police report followed. "Sutter County Police are cooperating with the FBI in the effort to apprehend the second of the escaped prisoners from Camp Beale. It is now thought that the escapee may have turned tail. He may be heading east."

"East?" said a board member.

"I suspect, sir, he will find that it is a longer road to Mexico than he thought."

Laughter.

"There's forests all the way to the state line. He will be difficult to find."

"He won't survive long without food or water."

Murmurs.

Maria watched Emilio from the corner of her eye, in case he got wriggly and needed restraining. But Emilio was frozen in place from sheer awe. He couldn't take his eyes off the giant flags at the head of the room—the American flag, and across from it the state flag, with "California Republic" in brown letters, and a bear walking across a patch of green against a white background.

The man from the *Appeal-Democrat* got busy taking notes.

After the excitement about the prisoner died down, voices droned on about leases and right-of-way and a vote to release an abandoned building on Plumas to the War Relocation Authority for administrative purposes.

Finally the gavel slammed down on the desk.

Miss Newman sat bolt upright.

The man with the gavel said, "Item number eight. Vote on playing field site. Request to defer and reallocate site for mixed-use purposes."

Maria heard two words. Playing field. That was all it

took. She sprang to her feet, waved her hand at the scary people behind the long polished desk, and cried out, "Wait! Wait! We need that ball field."

The ik-do twins squealed in astonishment. "Shh!" Connie warned.

To Maria's left, Papi was shaking his head, mouthing in Punjabi, finger to his lips: *Choop! Choop!* Too late.

The newspaper reporter sat up and began to scribble madly. Maria's wild self had stepped way over the line.

A firestorm of hoots and whistles and cries burst out from just about every person under twelve years old in the room. "Yeah!" "We're with her! She's right!" "We want our ball field!"

Boys and girls were together on this, since everyone would get to use that field. No more goatgrass burrs and gopher holes.

"Rats to mixed-up use!" Tim Singh's lispy voice was unmistakable.

The man with the gavel turned so red that Maria thought he was about to explode. He whacked the long desk as if he meant to crack it. He broke into an uncontrollable cough and his eyes ran with tears. The cough hacked and racked and choked him and he could not stop. A glass of water was rushed up to him on a little brass tray. This finally calmed him down.

Papi sank down in his seat and covered his face with his hands.

When the room was quiet again, the gavel man, his redness waning in shades, leaned over and looked directly at Maria. "Young lady," he said hoarsely. "I assure you that you will get the chance to speak."

Maria opened her mouth to say, *Thank you,* or *I'm sorry,* or both. But "No, no, no," said the man, so she shut it back up again.

"If," he continued, "you speak out of turn one more time, I promise you that I will have you summarily ejected from these chambers, so help me God. Do you understand?"

Maria murmured, "Yes, sir."

"Now, *siddown!*" snapped the man with the gavel, and she sat down, shaking, the bump on her head beginning to throb from too much excitement.

The board members talked among themselves. The original plan for the ball field had been approved some months ago, but no money had been allocated for it. There was a ballpark just across the line in Yuba County, after all, and was that not close enough?

It is not! Maria longed to protest, but she had the good sense to keep her lip buttoned.

In contrast, the mixed-use site was practical and useful. It would generate cement and metal work for local workmen. There would be a community center building and maybe even some shops. It would be good for local businesses. The five acres had already been deeded unconditionally to the county by Levee District 1 and the Farm Security Administration. The county could do as it wished with the land.

"It's no contest," said one of the men at the desk.

"At the very least, the ball field can be delayed, can it not?" asked another.

Maria listened, understanding only about every third word, but knowing that the future was in the hands of these five men sitting behind the desk. She didn't dare look up. Eventually silence settled. Maria felt someone's eyes on her, so she looked up in a panic, afraid she'd missed something.

She met the eyes of the man with the gavel. He said, "The chairman now invites comments from the floor."

Maria hesitated. She wasn't going to throw herself into this play now until she knew what it meant.

Miss Newman raised her hand.

Gavel Man said, "Ma'am?" and invited Miss Newman to speak her name and residence for the record and make a brief statement.

Miss Newman went up to the big desk and gave her name and address, so the clerk could write it down. Then she said, "Gentlemen, I teach school in this county, and I have been teaching our girls how to play ball. I would like to introduce my student, Maria Esperanza Singh, to open comments from students and their families."

And Miss Newman waved Maria up, just waved her right up to the three steps at the foot of the giant desk. She walked up those steps and found herself eye to eye with the men who sat behind the expanse of polished wood. Behind her was breathless silence, except for the scratching of the reporter's pencil and the clack-clack-clack of the clerk's typewriter.

Maria swallowed her nervousness in one gulp. "Sir," she began, then stopped. She cleared her throat, caught Gavel Man's eye. It held a faintly encouraging gleam.

"I'm in Miss Newman's fifth-grade class," she went on, "and I really want to play ball in a proper field, where she can teach us the rules just like in the leagues. Even if we don't have real teams yet, we can learn the game so when we're old enough, there will be teams we can play on." Her words picked up strength as she went on. "And thank you for listening to us kids, because normally no one asks us what we think about things."

They were listening all right. Even the typist had stopped clacking, her hands poised over the keyboard.

Miss Newman's words came flooding back to Maria, and suddenly they became *her* words, because now at last she understood what they meant. "We need to learn to speak up and be heard. So thank you for listening to us, because this is how things work in a democracy."

Gavel Man nodded at her. He almost looked kindly, so she kept on going. "So if we have a proper ball field, then one day . . . one day we can have proper teams and play real games and our families can all come and see us, and we can be . . . we can be . . ." The word hit her like a ball slamming into a catcher's mitt. "Proud," she said. "We can be proud. Everyone's got a right to feel that way sometimes."

Maria turned around. "Proud to be American," she whispered. She walked down the steps, shocked by the waves of applause that threatened to shut down the proceedings once again. Her knees were so wobbly it was a minor miracle she made it back to her seat at all.

Papi was staring at Maria as if *he* was witnessing a real live miracle. He put his arm around her as she sat back down. She was shaking.

Connie hugged her hard and whispered, "You knocked their socks off!"

Others got up to speak—parents, a few more of the children.

There were some objections. One man said he didn't see why the kids of Sutter County couldn't go to neighboring Wheatland to play. When pressed, he admitted he was not a local man but a visitor from San Francisco. He didn't know the field near Wheatland had been taken over by Wartime Civil Control for a holding center for enemy aliens. That had left it with pools of standing water and the rubble left from putting up a bunch of temporary buildings. Even the board of supervisors didn't object when the man was booed right out.

The supervisors talked about it for close to another hour. In the end, the vote was unanimous. The ball field was placed on the city's master plan, with immediate approval to seek ways to fund it.

CHAPTER TWENTY-NINE

The Stockton Temple

PERHAPS AFTER ALL, THE WORLD WAS STARTING TO turn a little faster in the right direction, because on Wednesday, the day after the county board meeting, the news broke everywhere that the war in Europe was over. The Germans had surrendered. It was only a matter of time, surely, before the Japanese would too, and then the war would *truly* be over.

The German prisoner who had escaped from Camp Beale had been found and returned. He claimed he was glad to be back, or at least that is what the paper reported. The *Appeal-Democrat* editorial wondered if he was happy to be in America instead of in Germany being bombed.

Maria had to stay home the remainder of the week because Papi, the nurse, and Mamá agreed that she could use the rest. Thankfully, she did not have to stay in bed all the time. She could get up and walk around a little, but she could not go out. Connie and Janie came by, bringing news. Practice was going well. Everyone missed Maria.

Emilio was staying over at the Khans' place after school until Papi walked over to pick him up at the end of each day, which was good because if he was home he would just bother Maria. Nobody, ever before in all her life, had paid such attention to keeping Maria rested.

The biggest surprise of all came on Friday morning.

Mamá said, "There's someone to see you."

"Who?" Maria said.

"You will never guess," said Mamá. And then who should walk in but Elizabeth. Elizabeth!

Maria nearly fell out of bed from shock.

At first they did not say anything to each other. Then Elizabeth started to say, "You know—" at the same time as Maria started to say, "I think—" and then they both stopped and coughed and looked anywhere except at each other.

Then Elizabeth said, "I want to say—" just as Maria said, "I really didn't—" and this time they did look at each other.

And what Maria saw was—a girl.

A girl with blonde hair instead of her own dark, and

blue eyes instead of her own brown. That's what. A girl who did not have a mamá. A girl whose daddy was bad-tempered and maybe he loved her and maybe he didn't, but everybody hated him. Maybe people had reasons for that—all those stories about a bad-tempered man with a gun couldn't be totally wrong—but surely stories were not reason enough to hate a person.

So instead of saying all these things that could not be said, Maria said instead, "You haven't gone to Sacramento yet?"

And Elizabeth said, "No. We're not leaving until July. I'm going to play in that game."

"Game? What game?"

"The one we're going to play at the end of the month."

"We are?" Maria said.

"In Stockton. There's a team of girls there."

Stockton! A game? Maria was flabbergasted.

Then Elizabeth said, "I'm sorry. You got hurt really bad. I didn't mean that. Well, maybe I did—people were mean to us, and then when you broke that window I was so angry . . . ."

Maria said, "It was a mistake. The window, I mean. Really, it was. And I'm sorry about that."

They looked away from each other again, all the sorries being said. Pretty soon Elizabeth left, and Maria thought, in a daze, *Maybe we can be friends. Maybe such a thing is possible.*

By the afternoon, Maria said, "Mamá, I will go crazy if I have to stay in the house for one minute longer."

She was surprised when Mamá said, "Well, then, get dressed. Get ready."

"Really? Where are we going?"

"Papi will tell you," said Mamá mysteriously.

And there was Papi, home early, wiping the dirt off his boots, and calling, "Maria! Emilio! We're going to the gurudwara!"

"What's that?" asked Emilio.

"The Sikh temple," Papi replied.

"In Stockton?" Maria said.

"Where do you think?" Mamá slicked Emilio's hair down in the back where it stuck up. "He's taking us all to India?"

"India?" Maria said, trying to mimic Harriet's voice from Mamá's favorite radio show. "How's Papi going to take us across the ocean in his truck?"

"Funny," said Papi. "No, India is coming to the Stockton Sikh Temple today, just for us."

"India?" Emilio's mouth fell open.

"An important visitor," Papi said, "is coming to speak to us all about India's independence."

"Independence?" Maria said. "From the Angrez?"

"Aho," said Papi. The visitor was a lady, it seemed. The papers called her Madame Pandit. She was the sister of a famous man, Mr. Nehru, whose name often rushed past in radio news reports about India.

Further wonders were to come. When they all got ready and piled into the cab of the truck, Maria saw that over his ordinary haircut, Papi had put on his royal-blue turban.

"Is your hair going to grow back, Papi?" Emilio asked.

"No, puttar," Papi said. "My turban is just a sign of respect."

"Because India's coming to America today?" Maria asked.

Papi laughed out loud and hit the gas pedal. "Very good." The scenery whizzed by.

"That's not thirty-five," Mamá warned. "You slow down, or we'll be talking to the cops today before we ever hear a single word out of that important lady."

"Worse," Papi said, and he slowed down. "I'll lose my gas coupons."

•••

Madame Vijaya Lakshmi Pandit had short silver-streaked hair. She stood on the front steps of the temple in her Indian sari, which was draped around her in soft pleats over a sleeveless blouse.

Maria longed to touch the sari—it was so creamy-beautiful with its brick-red border and its pleated front. Before Madame Pandit spoke to the crowd assembled in her honor, someone from the temple placed a garland of flowers around her neck. She graciously kept it there for the rest of the evening, although it looked heavy and a little uncomfortable. In an unexpectedly soft voice, she thanked the temple committee for inviting her, and the people of Stockton and California who were hosting her visit.

Papi nudged Maria and Emilio up, up, up, until they were standing only a few feet away from the distinguished guest. She talked about the war and how India was determined to find her way to freedom peacefully. "Thanks to the inspiration of Gandhiji and the leaders of our struggle," she said, "we are determined to take our place without violence in the ranks of free nations. Many have gone to jail in our cause. Many have given up everything they possessed to join the freedom struggle. We ask you to donate generously.

Please support us now." Soft as they were, delicately spoken, her words held the crowd in silence. Applause scattered respectfully at her conclusion.

Questions followed. When did she think India's independence would become a reality? Next year? The year after?

"I can't say," she replied.

Would India continue to support Britain's war effort in the Pacific if she were granted independence?

"It is not for me to make any such guarantees," she said, "but we are allies in the war against fascism and imperialism."

"And what of the Indians in America?" someone asked. "When will they be granted the right to be full citizens in this great nation?"

Madame Pandit smiled, and the electric lights shining down on her silver hair gave it the look of a halo, dazzling Maria for a moment before she focused again on the light, sweet voice. "I wish you all diligence and persistence in your efforts," she said. "Yours is a just cause, and in the end, just causes must prevail."

Thunderous applause ended the address before the crowd began to make its way into the temple, removing shoes at the door and covering their heads with handkerchiefs and scarves. Some of the men wore turbans, even though, like Papi, many were clean-shaven.

Slap, slap! Emilio loved to smack his bare feet upon the floor. At one end of the room sat an elder with a big book open in front of him. People gathered around, finding places to sit in the clusters of chairs arranged around the great hall, or on the floor in front. The elder began to recite from the book, singsonging the words, while a man showed a boy about Emilio's age how to catch the rhythm on twin tabla drums.

One-two-three! went the boy's fingers marking the beat. One-two-three, one-two-three-four! Others stood on either side of the holy book, swishing over it something that looked like a big soft white beard attached to a silver handle. They stirred the air gently over the book, and over the elder reading from it in his shaky old-man voice.

Maria recognized that face and voice. "Papi, that's Bauji!"

It was. Janie and her mother and sister were there too, as were the Khans and several other adha-adha families from around the county. The women were mostly Mexican, a few Anglos among them, and only one who had come from India, before 1923 when the laws forbade it. Unlike the

Mexican wives, who all wore dresses, this older lady wore loose pants with a long tunic over them and she covered her head and shoulders with a long, gauzy scarf.

After the reading, the uncles sang. Madame Pandit sat with the crowd, sat right there on a folding chair along with everyone else and listened to the singing. Some of the words repeated themselves, the same way that words in the Mass were repeated at the Catholic church. When the uncles came to those repeating bits, Maria found that she could join in, Papi's words coming easily to her tongue. "Waheguru, waheguru, waheguru satnaam." She sang along, delighted to catch the refrain each time it rose again between stanzas.

After the singing, everyone went out again and put their shoes back on. The uncles milled around and talked to each other, and people lined up to greet Madame Pandit. "Come on," said Papi, and they joined the line.

By the time they got to the head of it, Emilio was transfixed by the flags behind the visitor. The Stars and Stripes stood to the left. Directly behind Madame Pandit was the flag of the temple, with the golden symbol of the Sikh religion on it—crossed swords with another kind of double-edged blade up the middle in front of a circle. But it was the third flag, the one on the right, that had arrested Emilio's attention.

Papi was talking to Madame Pandit now, and introducing his wife and his children to her. Mamá shook her hand and Maria did too—it was a soft hand with a surprisingly firm grip—but Emilio was still staring at that flag.

Papi murmured excuses for his distracted son, but Madame Pandit bent down until she was eye level with Emilio. "Would you like to take a closer look?" she said.

He nodded, speechless.

"That's the flag of the Indian National Congress," she said. "See?" She took an end of it in her hand, shaking its folds loose so Emilio could look at its saffron and green with a white band between them. "That's a spinning wheel," she said, pointing to two wheel-like circles in the middle of the white band, joined by loops of thread. "It's Gandhiji's symbol for self-reliance. We hope that one day these colors will stand for an independent India."

"Who's Gandhiji?" Maria asked Papi when they had moved on and the next people in line were shaking the lady's hand.

"All of India follows him," was all that Papi would say, feeling first in one pocket and then another as if he'd forgotten something.

"What do you need?" Mamá asked.

"My wallet," said Papi. He found it and pulled out a five-dollar bill.

Five dollars! That was a week's worth of dry goods—tea and coffee, flour and sugar. Papi placed it in a collection plate set on a stand against the wall.

"Why's Papi giving—?" Emilio began, and stopped when he met Mamá's eye.

"But why?" he whispered to Maria.

"For the people in India," Maria told him. "So they can be free."

"That's good," Emilio said offhandedly.

"Very good," she assured him. For just one minute she felt them all folded into Papi's world with that five-dollar bill. As if they were wrapped in an instant, with Papi's thoughts, around that distant land, even while his body was here and his hand rested on Emilio's shoulder.

And now there was one more line left to stand in, the line for kara-parshad. Today it was dished up on squares of newspaper with tin spoons. The spoonfuls went down warm and tender, bursting with sweet goodness.

"Papi," said Maria as they drove back home at the end of this unexpected outing. "You ever feel sad that your big gold temple in India is so far away?"

Papi said, "What's to be sad about?"

"You can't go see it anytime you want to," Maria said.

Papi smiled. "My family is here. My life is here."

She still carried the thrumming of drums and voices inside her. These same songs, this same beat—how would it be, sung and drummed and felt in a big, big church-like space? She imagined Papi's temple with its golden dome. It stood in the middle of a great, flat lake, all edged with the softness of its fairy-tale distance.

She dared, even, to wonder, *Could it be . . . ? Could it ever happen that one day I might go all the way to the province of Punjab in faraway India, and see Papi's big temple with the roof of gold?* The very idea made her mind take wing.

I would come back, of course, she thought, *back to Sutter County, back home.* Still, for an instant, the idea of seeing that kind of story place with her own eyes staggered her.

But Papi said, "All the God you ever need, you carry in your heart."

It was not until they had gone past the Yuba City limits and were halfway to the Feather River Bridge that the jumble in Maria's mind—independence India sari kara-parshad singing Golden Temple just cause five-dollar bill—all came together with a resounding clang and grew into a bold new idea.

Papi was just turning off Plumas Avenue when the idea hit Maria. Should she share it? She didn't know whether it was crazy or made any sense. But it couldn't hurt, could it? There weren't any other options. She decided to tell him.

"Papi!" Maria cried.

Startled, Papi mistimed the gear, causing a dreadful grinding noise and making Mamá clutch at her seat.

When he recovered, Papi said, "Don't do that again. What's the matter?"

"Papi," Maria said, "I'm a citizen. And Emilio is too."

"Yes. So?"

"So we could buy that land for you. Couldn't we? If we had money?"

Papi swerved to miss a suicidal rabbit scampering in front of the truck.

Maria said, "I'm just saying. But we don't have any money and we're not old enough. But Mamá—"

Mamá said, slowly, "What?"

Maria said, "If I could buy that land for us, I would. That's all."

Suddenly, Mamá turned and looked at Maria with her

eyes all narrow as if she had just thought of something and was afraid the thought would run away from her.

"What?" said Maria. "Do you know what I'm saying? Couldn't Papi just say . . . ?"

"That the land is in your names?" said Mamá slowly.

"Or yours?" Maria said. "We are citizens. Mamá is a citizen too, right?"

"Yes, but I can't own land, Maria," Mamá said.

"A married woman's legal status is that of her husband," Papi said gloomily. "Your Mamá came down in the world by marrying me."

"So then us, Papi? Me and Emilio. Could you not put it in our names?"

Under his breath Papi began to sing.

"Couldn't you?" Maria said. "Is it allowed?"

"Hmm," said Papi. "I'm thinking, I'm thinking."

He was singing while he thought. "Waheguru waheguru," Papi was singing. "Waheguru satnaam." Mamá crossed herself. There were many ways to praise the Lord for sending a really good idea into a girl's mind.

CHAPTER THIRTY

New Tomorrow

BACK HOME AT LAST FROM THE TEMPLE, MARIA AND Emilio sat on the steps, looking at Tía Manuela's latest, newly arrived postcard. It was a picture of the Hollywood Bowl, a gigantic amphitheater in LA.

This is what Tía Manuela's message said:

Maria, your mamá called me—I hope you're better. Keep on keeping on.

Love, Tía M.

Mamá called Tía Manuela? On the telephone? That meant she had to go into town and book a call through the operator at the post office, because phone lines, like indoor plumbing, had yet to make their way from the city limits to the farmhouses. Only a real crisis could move Mamá to make a phone call.

A flock of geese bobbed their way through the sky in an off-center vee.

"Maria," Emilio said.

"Hmm?"

"Look. Are they going south?"

"The geese? Nah, too early."

"Don't they always fly south?"

"How can that be, Emilio?" Maria said. "They have to come back, right? So then they fly north, don't they?"

"Oh," he said, crestfallen.

"They'll go in the winter," she said. "To Mexico."

"How about now?"

"Now? I don't know."

"It's an awful long way to Mexico, isn't it?"

"Mamá came all the way," Maria said. "And Papi did too. Longer, even."

"That's different," Emilio said, flatly certain. "Mamá and Papi are not geese. We are not geese."

Silly things can set a person laughing. At first Emilio sat there quite seriously, but when Maria started laughing, he too began to giggle. Laughter broke the dread of the days just past and shaped a new tomorrow starting at that very minute. It shimmered the outlines of the grass and the rocks and the outhouse and the bathhouse, and the beans and tomatoes in the vegetable garden.

They laughed so hard they both had to clutch their sides. Maria found herself wiping her eyes, dashing away the moisture that lurked too close behind.

Maria was coming in from the outhouse on Saturday morning when all kinds of commotion broke out at the front door. Mamá was walking toward the house. In her hand was the bottle of milk she had just gotten from the milk van.

"Special delivery?" Papi was saying to the mailman, who stood at the door holding a package wrapped in brown paper. "We were not expecting any special delivery."

The man at the door was saying he was quite sure it was for this address. Was this not 216-B Farm Road?

Papi said maybe there was some mistake and the package was intended for 216-A. "Becker," he said. "Just up that way."

Which was when Mamá, with the bottle of milk still in her hand, almost knocked Maria over in her haste to get to Papi before he sent the special Saturday mail delivery man packing in his half-ton postal truck. "No, no, Kartar, it is for us, it's for—" Mamá set the milk down hastily before it went pitching into the grass.

"Becker," Papi said impatiently. "It must be for Becker."

"That's what I been trying to tell you, sir," said the mailman. "Last name on this package is Singh. Miss Maria Esperanza Singh."

"Me?" Maria cried, stunned.

"Here you go, miss." The mailman handed the package over. "Hope you like what's in it." He got away as fast as he could, his creaky black mail truck leaving a cloud of dust in its wake.

"It's from the Broadway!" Maria stared at the label. "In LA? Who would send me . . . ?"

"That's a big store! Oh, m'ijita, open it quickly." Mamá was almost dancing with excitement.

"Will someone tell me what's all this?" said Papi.

But when Maria had ripped through the brown paper envelope and the layers of tissue inside to find the enclosed gift card and the gift itself, no explaining was needed at all.

"From Tía Manuela," Maria whispered. "A baseball cap." It was a beauty of a cap, black with a short visor and rayon braid around the edge. Just like the women in the big league wore. Maria put it on and it fit, soft and easy.

CHAPTER THIRTY-ONE

Invitations

MARIA DECIDED SHE WOULD NEVER IN A HUNDRED years forget how it felt to wear her new cap to practice. No one made a fuss. They all noticed, though. She could tell from the smiles flashing back and forth. Connie gave a V for Victory sign that made Maria want to jump sky-high. Victory was in the air, what with the war ending in Europe and everyone already prepared to give thanks for peace, even if a full peace was yet to come.

Over the following week, Mamá was full of high spirits. She arranged for Janie's sister, Gloria, to bring Emilio home so Maria could stay back for practice. She saved extra eggs to make for breakfast before Maria left for school.

School days came and went. Practice grew tougher and longer.

Halfway through the next week, Miss Newman said, "We're not going to have time to get proper uniforms made before the game, but maybe we can get caps."

That made Connie yell, "Like Maria's beanie!"

Miss Newman took a close look at Maria's cap, sent by Tía Manuela all the way from LA. "Very nice," she said. "I'd better start asking around for sewing volunteers. We could make up a batch just like this, I think."

"We're going to play for real!" "When's the game, Miss Newman?"

Whee-eep! went Miss Newman's whistle. "We have been invited to a friendly game before the end of the school year," Miss Newman said, unfolding an official-looking letter. "By a new girls' team that has just formed in Stockton. The Ravens."

"When?" Maria said.

"On Saturday the twenty-sixth of May."

Everyone cheered and clapped, even the boys, who were there with bats and gloves in hand and a kind of wary look in their eyes.

"Hey! We need a name for our team!" Janie said.

"Any suggestions?" asked Miss Newman.

Suggestions broke out all over. "We should have a bird name too, like them."

"Eagles?"

"Magpies?"

"Seagulls?" said Dot. Her and Lucy's auntie lived near Seattle, so they had once spent a summer there chasing seagulls on cold, wet beaches.

"Magpies?" Miss Newman said. "You know, of course, that yellow-billed magpies are special to our part of the state."

" 'Magpies' sounds weird."

"Yeah, but how about Yellowbills?"

"Larks?" "Swallows?"

They voted with a show of hands and Yellowbills it was. A cheer went up.

Elizabeth even said something that was practically friendly. At least, that's what Maria thought it was meant to be. Elizabeth said, "You could turn your cap into a halfway decent Yellowbill, Maria, with a little bit of felt and some glue."

"I could," Maria said. Maybe Elizabeth was turning

into a halfway decent person now before Maria's eyes. Or maybe the old Maria would have read that comment as an insult about her cap, only now she was reading other people differently.

Miss Newman tucked the letter into her pocket. "Well—there you are, girls. We have a game coming up. These gentlemen are here to help us. What are we going to do?"

"Play ball!" they all yelled, even the gentlemen.

"Then what are you waiting for?" Miss Newman cried. "Let's go, go, go!"

They started with the boys on the field and the girls batting. Connie was a good hitter, and Janie too. And when Maria batted, she got the ball past the shortstop and made it easily to third base. The boys looked a bit uneasy. They laughed and joked a little too loudly because maybe they weren't sure they liked it so well when a girl got good.

Then the boys batted. Maria's radio announcer voice ran the plays in her mind. *Mondo's batting—first pitch to Maria at shortstop, she fields it cleanly, fires it at first. Ought to be a breeze.*

Elizabeth at first base. Drops the ball.

"Use both hands," Miss Newman reminded them.

Next pitch Mondo's swinging, and the ball flies out to

Elizabeth; she stands with her gloved hand stretched out. Oh!
Oh! She mistimes it. She closes that glove too soon, too soon.
The ball bounces off her closed hand.

"Wait for the ball," Miss Newman called.

Mondo makes it to first and Tim and the others are
jumping up and down cheering him like mad.

Next pitch. "I've got it, I've got it!" said Elizabeth.

Never mind. Radio announcer Maria saw it coming. *A*
pop fly—it pops into Elizabeth's glove and rolls right out!

Everyone groaned. Even the boys groaned, and you'd
think they'd have been happy. "That was an easy one," Miss
Newman said. "What happened?"

"Come on, Elizabeth!" Maria and Janie cried together.

At that moment Maria saw someone standing a little
apart from the crowd of kids and parents who often
gathered to see Miss Newman's girls practice. Cap over
his face, feet planted squarely, hands in the pockets of his
overalls. Maria thought she was going to fall down in a heap
from astonishment.

Maybe it meant nothing. It could be purely coincidence.
It must be. It was unthinkable that anything she said could
have persuaded that grumpy, bad-tempered man to be
here.

Still, who would have thought it? Mr. Arnold Becker himself, come to see his daughter practice.

"Why, there's your father, Elizabeth," Connie said.

Elizabeth looked up, nodding. "I know."

"He came to see you play," Maria said.

Elizabeth sighed. She said, "I can't ever do anything right for him, can I?"

Maria said, "Never mind. You will do it right, and he will see you." And like Papi, she added, "Believe it."

Mamá's good spirits were still bubbling like a pot of beans when Maria got home after practice. Papi had gone to the bank and to the county clerk's office, Mamá said. When he returned he had a sheaf of papers with him. He spread them out on the kitchen table and pored over them. "I wish I could read better," he said.

"What do you think?" Mamá said. "Can we do it?"

"I don't understand everything. But we have the money, and the county clerk's office said they will stamp the papers. It's legal, Hortensia!"

"What does legal mean?" said Emilio, double-twirling his penny and catching it on the back of his hand.

"When did you learn to do that?" Maria said.

"Papi taught me," said Emilio. "What's happening?"

She told him. "Papi's going to buy the farm from Mr. Becker. Only he's going to make the papers say it's in our names, yours and mine."

"Oh." Emilio looked disappointed. "Is that all?"

The land was to be registered in the children's names, as they were American citizens. Mamá was a citizen too, but under the law, that terrible law that was so slow to change, she'd given up her right to own land when she married Papi.

Papi said, "I've invited the lawyer to dinner tonight, is that all right?"

"Is he the one who comes to Ahmed's restaurant?" Mamá asked.

"That's the one," Papi said. That lawyer, it turned out, had once traveled by ship all the way to India, and was a frequent patron of the restaurant.

"Do we have any eggs?" Papi asked. "Ahmed says he's fond of egg curry."

"Government pickup doesn't come till tomorrow," Mamá said. She looked in the icebox. "We got eight left. My egg curry's not so good, Kartar."

"You're always saying no one ever gets good without trying, Mamá." Maria grinned.

"Serves me right," said Mamá. "I've raised a girl with a big mouth!"

The lawyer recommended by Ahmed Uncle stopped by later that evening. Mamá's egg curry was a pot of pure, spiced joy.

The children ate early—so as not to get in the way—but Maria eavesdropped shamelessly, and was impressed.

"Convincing buyer . . . lucrative . . . proof." The lawyer, Mr. Markham, spouted these and other words through puffs of his pipe. He spread out a great big plan from the county surveyor's office onto the kitchen table, and pointed out parts of it to Papi.

Before he left, Mr. Markham said, "You be firm now. You're within your rights."

Within your rights. Words with weight, words that meant what they said. They were words that contained promises you might even be able to trust.

CHAPTER THIRTY-TWO

Yellowbills versus Ravens

THE LAST SATURDAY IN MAY DAWNED BRIGHT AS A picture postcard. True, the newspapers still reported that Japan was burning beneath American bombs, but Germany had been defeated and people were glad to be thinking of something other than the war. Doña Elena had farmed caps out to Mamá and the aunties, and there were eleven black-and-yellow beanies in the bus that jolted the Yellowbills south to Stockton for the game.

The San Joaquin County sheriff, Tom Trapp, gave a long speech. "Baseball is a sport that is national in scope," he said, making his voice ring out the way important people's voices are supposed to do, "and it is a matter of prestige and pride for us that it is now being played by our modern girls in our own county."

He went on in this vein for several minutes. When everyone thought he was done and began to clap, it seemed to give him new wind. He added some more ideas about hard work and perseverance. The crowd was so pleased when he finally stopped that they burst into enthusiastic applause, after which he spent a long time tipping his hat to the people he assumed admired him.

The Yellowbills had gathered, their black cloth beanies sporting bright yellow visors. Janie ran her finger along the inside and Maria grinned at her. Her own cap was soft and comfortable on the inside, but everyone else's seams itched a little from too much of Doña Elena's trademark starch.

Picnics had started to spread out all over the edge of the field. The crowds were collecting. Gramps Anderson had set up a little booth selling Spam sandwiches and Cracker Jack. The sun, which had been hiding behind clouds all morning, suddenly poured its rays out upon the entire company. It was as if the county was carrying all its hope for the ending of the war into this game.

The sheriff came on over and wanted to know, "What's next? Are we ready to play some ball?"

"Ready, girls?" said Miss Newman.

Everyone cheered as the national anthem started up.

The Yellowbills and the Ravens and the whole crowd joined in, hands on hearts, while a local church choir trilled "The Star-Spangled Banner" all the way to ". . . the hooooome of the braaaaaaaaaave." That was a lot of people singing. A crowd. There had to be sixty or seventy people who had come to see the girls play.

A minister from a church in town said a prayer, and Monsignor Gonzales said a prayer, and both of them were about peace and thankfulness, as all prayers had come to be.

The sheriff doubled as umpire. He flipped a coin. The Yellowbills won the toss and got to be the home team. The game began with the Ravens up to bat first and Janie at shortstop. Maria pitching, Connie catching, Elizabeth at first base, Suze at second, and Lucy at third. There were four in the outfield—Dot, Milly, Sal, and Joyce.

Maria's first pitch was nice and fast, right down the middle. The batter swung and missed. "Stee-rike one!" cried the sheriff. He winked at the crowd and said, to anyone willing to listen, "Sorry. I've always wanted to say that."

"Go, girls," Miss Newman yelled.

Maria pitched again.

"Good pitch, Maria!" It was Connie.

"You can do it!" Dot yelled.

The muscles in Maria's right shoulder contracted. She grimaced. She hadn't had that pain since she was home in bed, and she'd thought it was gone. She ignored it. In her mind, she switched Radio Maria on.

It's a fastball over the outside edge of the plate. The batter swings, touches the ball. Ump calls a foul ball. Next pitch—a soft liner pops up in the air. Shortstop catches the ball and the batter's out! Shortstop throws the ball back to the pitcher. Maria's inner announcer filled up with sunshine and goodwill and with a game that played out like a story.

The Yellowbills made it through the first half of the inning with the Ravens held to no runs.

The girls streamed back into the dugout. "All right," Miss Newman said. "Let's get some runs on the board."

The bottom of the inning ended with Yellowbills 1, Ravens 0. The score went back and forth—first the Yellowbills leading, then the Ravens, then the Yellowbills again.

At the top of the fourth, the Yellowbills were out in the field once more, with some players switching positions. Miss Newman had Connie relieve Maria at pitching, to give that shoulder a rest. "Give it to 'em, Connie," Miss Newman said. "Janie, you're on second. Suze, you're shortstop. Go get 'em, girls!"

On the bench, Maria kept her inner commentary running. *Connie pitches and it's a fastball. She's a leftie. See that stance? She is good. Batter swings. Swings over top of the ball. Misses. The ball hits the ground just behind the plate. That's a strike.* It helped not to think about that slight sharp pain somewhere beneath her shoulder blade.

"Give them another one!" someone called from the crowd.

The second pitch was right on the money again, but this time the batter was looking for another fastball. Connie put it right where the Ravens' batter wanted it. The batter made solid contact.

The ball goes straight, a line drive between first and second. Janie makes a play to her left. She stumbles, overreaches, falls.

"Oh no, Janie!" Maria called. But Janie had done what you were never supposed to do when you fell. She'd put her arm out to brace her fall, and taken it right on the wrist. She cried out in pain.

Sheriff called time.

Janie's holding her wrist with her other hand and wincing in pain. Her mother runs up to help her off the field. That was not what Maria's inner commentator wanted to say, but it was true.

What were they going to do now?

Miss Newman huddled with them. "Maria? Second base? Can you manage?"

Maria nodded. She could. She would. She had to. Then it was back to play, Maria on second and Didi, off the bench at last, in the outfield.

"We're ready to go," Miss Newman called.

"You sure?" asked the sheriff.

Miss Newman said, "We're sure."

Despite everything, the magic was back. Fly balls landed in Maria's glove as if heaven itself was sending them there. She fielded the grounders. She was a whirlwind. She snapped those balls up as they came. The Yellowbills made it to the bottom of the sixth, tied with the Ravens, 6–6.

Top of the seventh, the Ravens scored and now the board read 7–6.

Dot was the next up to bat. The girls cheered. "Dot! Dot! Dotty!"

"Watch the ball," said Miss Newman.

The ball flew. Dot swung.

"Stee-rike one!"

The cheering grew louder.

Next ball. Dot swung again. "Stee-rike two!" The sheriff could hardly contain himself.

Dot gripped the bat, stared out. The third pitch was right down the center. She cracked it for a line drive that went between first and second all the way to right field. She ran to first.

The screaming and cheering grew frantic.

"We've got to get her home," said Miss Newman.

Lucy was up next. She slammed the first pitch right over the shortstop's head and ran to first. Dot was already halfway to second by the time the left fielder picked up the ball and fired it to second base.

"Safe all around," called Miss Newman. She turned to Maria. "Can you do it?"

Maria looked up. There were Papi and Mamá and Emilio, waving at her. And who was that? Among the milling crowds, Maria saw someone else. Tía Manuela had arrived late, but she'd made it all the way from Los Angeles to see Maria play.

"Maria," said Miss Newman.

"Ready," said Maria. She reached for the bat.

The first pitch was wide. "Ball one!"

The second one was way inside. She jumped back.

Maria watched to see what the third pitch would be.

She swung, but it was a little late. And what was happening to her shoulder? Oh no! The pain intensified.

"Strike one!"

Eye on the ball, Maria. She flexed the muscles in her neck and shoulders. All the time she had to spend in bed had made her weak, when she should have been practicing. The shoulder gave a sharp twinge.

The moment the next pitch flew out, Maria knew it was too low.

"Ball three!" Sheriff called.

"Come on, Maria!" Miss Newman called. "You know what to do." When the count was three balls and one strike, it was all up to the pitcher. A ball, and she'd walk. A strike, and she'd still be fine. She still had one more strike to go.

The pitcher let it fly. It was perfect. A perfect ball, just for Maria.

But at the last minute, the ball curved. Maria swung with all her might. She wanted to slam it. But something was terribly wrong. Her shoulder felt as if lightning had struck it and was about to burn it out. She clutched that bat and willed herself to forget the pain.

She missed it completely. The crowd groaned.

"Strike two!"

"Maria! Maree-a!" the girls yelled. She heard all their voices, joining together. She loved them all and she tried her best to block them out. Was Papi's voice in there? Emilio's? She steeled herself.

Miss Newman called, "Come on, Maria. You can do it!"

Maria clenched her teeth. Over the pain, she pulled back. She was ready.

The pitcher took her stance. She gripped the ball. She hurled it. The ball came straight and true.

Without even thinking, Maria stepped in and swung. Every muscle in her body aimed at that ball. Crack! Leather met wood.

Maria dropped the bat and took off for first. It was a hard hit, a line drive just inside the third base line. Dot scored easily from third.

Elizabeth took off from first.

The Ravens left fielder had to cover a lot of ground to get that ball.

Elizabeth rounded second and was well on her way to third. The ball made it all the way to the fence. Elizabeth kept on going.

The fielder makes a play for the ball. The throw home is a little wide and a little late. Elizabeth scores, she scores! The team rips onto the field and now everyone's hugging everyone! The crowd goes nuts.

Maria's heart thudded like a marching drum. *We won, we won, we won! We did it. All together, we did it.* The together part was purely unbelievable.

"We did it! We did it! We won!" Connie and Janie and even quiet Lucy were all shrieking so loudly people could probably hear them back by the Feather River Bridge.

"Maria! I saw you play! I saw you, I saw you!" Emilio was racing around her in circles, dizzy with delight.

"You did it, 'jita!" Tía Manuela hugged her. "It was your hit that did it."

Papi was staring at Maria as if she'd suddenly grown wings. He said, "Meri beti," and she was. She was his girl all right and he was proud of her.

"Oh, Papi." Papi circled her with a big warm hug. He didn't miss that she flinched when his arm touched her right shoulder. "Have you hurt it?"

"It's all right." The muscles clenched. She tried to hold still. It would get better.

"Look, Maria!" Emilio clutched something small and blue in his hand. "Papi got me my stamp and you won! All in one day!"

Maria laughed.

"And guess what else?" Emilio said. "Guess."

"I can't," she said. "You tell me."

"Papi's telling stories again," Emilio shouted in joy. "He told me one in the car on the way here. About a hen who laid an egg in the roof of Papi's house, back when he was a boy in India!"

Maria looked at Papi, and Papi pretended he had a cough, although what he had to hide might have been a smile instead. Maria looked at Mamá. Mamá lifted her hands in the air in a don't ask me gesture.

And here was Arnold Becker, and he was talking to them as if they were real people. He still had eyes of glass. That would not change. But he did not look so harshly at his daughter. And she did not frown so much. Small things like that could have the odd effect of making a bright day seem even brighter.

The world, it seemed, had stopped in its tracks, looked around itself, and changed direction. One day the war would be over. One day the people who were scattered on its account would come back, at least some of them would. Men who went to the front, and the Japanese people who were sent away. Sally and Eddie and Sam, the Yamates and the Ebiharas and all those people whose faces Maria could hardly even remember anymore. She hoped they'd come back.

Now that change was in the air, all things were possible, were they not? Maybe one day they would have a water connection to the house and Mamá's dream of indoor plumbing would come true. And one day, in Yuba City, California, there would be a ball field where girls and boys could play.

One day—Madame Pandit was surely right—the laws in two lands would change. Papi would become a citizen of America, and India would be free. Could a person be a citizen of more than one country? *There is so much,* she thought, *that I do not know.*

In the meantime, there was this day, and blessed it was, down to the last aching muscle. Waheguru, Maria thought, and crossed herself in gratitude.

The History Behind Maria's Story

The characters in this book are fictional, but families like Maria's did live in California's Sutter and Yuba Counties. Men from Punjab, India, came to California as farm workers, and many of them married women from Mexico. Descendants of these so-called Mexican-Hindu families still live in California today. In fact, most of the men were not of the Hindu religion. They were either Sikh or Muslim. The word "Hindu" at the time simply meant "people of Hindustan," which was another name for India.

In 1945, immigrants from the Indian subcontinent were not allowed to become citizens of the United States of America. In some states they could not own land. Some Punjabi men like Papi bought land in their children's names, as the children were US citizens by birth. The parents then took care of the land until their children were old enough to farm it themselves. An Act of Congress in 1946, the Luce-Celler Act, allowed people from India to enter the United

States once again as immigrants who were eligible to apply for citizenship.

By California law, people of different races could not marry. Punjabi men and Mexican women sometimes persuaded the county clerks to register their marriages by stating that they both belonged to the same race—"brown."

Children in families like Maria's were mostly raised Catholic, although many of the descendants still remember stories they heard from their fathers' religious traditions. The parents sometimes disagreed about how best to raise their daughters—whether the girls should date, for example, or wear pants!

In 1945, the American flag had forty-eight stars because Alaska and Hawaii hadn't yet joined the Union. The pledge of allegiance did not yet contain the words "under God."

The Little League was formed in 1938, but it was only for boys. Girls didn't join until 1974. Stories of women and girls playing ball, however, go as far back as the late 1800s. In 1945, girls in Yuba City played softball. That year, the official softball rulebook called for ten players on a team, with four in the outfield. Games consisted of seven innings. Sliding and stealing bases were not allowed. Today, in Yuba City, California, there are plenty of places, including a major sports complex, where young people can play softball.

On the other side of the world, at the time of this story, India was still ruled by the British. Vijaya Lakshmi Pandit, who later became India's first ambassador to the United Nations, did in fact visit the Sikh temple in Stockton, California, to seek money and support for India's independence movement.

India became free in 1947, two years after the end of World War II.

Acknowledgments

The kindness of many people helped make this book possible. My deepest thanks to Ali Rasul, Tamara English, Joseph Mallobox, Danny Mallobox Sr., Ruth Mallobox Silva, Lupe Saldana, and Stella and Ralie Singh for their generous gifts of stories and of their time. Thanks as well to Amrita Singh Hauser and Nicky Singh. I owe a special debt of gratitude to the late Ted Sibia. Ted encouraged me to write this story. I'm only sorry he passed away before its publication.

Chitra Banerjee Divakaruni's poetry collection, *Leaving Yuba City*, helped lead me to this work. So did Jayasri Majumdar Hart's documentary film, *Roots in the Sand*.

I'm grateful to those who read my many drafts: Anjali Banerjee, Audrey Couloumbis, Stephanie Farrow, the late Lucy Hampson, Katherine Hauth, Betsy James, Mark Karlins, Vaunda Micheaux Nelson, and Caroline Starr Rose. Kristine Ashworth and Stanley Falconer were my amazing softball coaches. Shauna Singh Baldwin and Guadalupe Garcia McCall helped me integrate the story's complicated cultural layers.

Thanks to students in my writers.com classes and to colleagues and students in the Writing for Children and Young Adults MFA program at Vermont College of Fine Arts.

Finally, heartfelt thanks to Louise May for her belief in this project, and to Stacy Whitman, for helping me bring its history and heart to the page.